No Love Lost

M. Vaden

Copyright © 2023 by Mariah Vaden

All rights reserved. No part of this publication may be reproduced, stored or transmitted in any form or by any means, electronic, mechanical, photocopying, recording, scanning, or otherwise without written permission from the publisher. It is illegal to copy this book, post it to a website, or distribute it by any other means without permission.

This novel is entirely a work of fiction. The names, characters and incidents portrayed in it are the work of the author's imagination. Any resemblance to actual persons, living or dead, events or localities is entirely coincidental.

First edition

This book was professionally typeset on Reedsy. Find out more at reedsy.com

Contents

Acknowledgement		v
1	Violet	1
2	Violet	7
3	Violet	14
4	Violet	19
5	Vincenzo	23
6	Violet	30
7	Vincenzo	37
8	Violet	43
9	Violet	50
10	Vincenzo	57
11	Violet	66
12	Vincenzo	69
13	Violet	75
14	Violet	82
15	Vincenzo	86
16	Violet	90
17	Vincenzo	95
18	Violet	99
19	Vincenzo	105
20	Violet	108
21	Vincenzo	113
22	Violet	121
23	Vincenzo	125

24	Violet	130
25	Vincenzo	133
26	Violet	137
27	Violet	140
28	Vincenzo	144
29	Violet	147
30	Vincenzo	152
31	Violet	158
32	Vincenzo	163
33	Violet	166
34	Vincenzo	173
35	Violet	178
36	Enzo	184
37	Vincenzo	188
38	Violet	189
39	Vincenzo	199
40	Violet	203
41	Vincenzo	207

Acknowledgement

This book contains explicit scenes that may be shocking or triggering to some. Below is a list of 'trigger warnings'. Some may be considered spoilers. TW included but not limited to: Suicide, PTSD, overdose, paranoia/anxiety, Non-con, dub-con, Sexual assault, Grooming, Death of a sibling, Human Trafficking, Kidnapping, Stalking, Cheating (not between FMC & MMC), Rape, Praise, BDSM, Breeding, Birth control disturbance, Primal play, Mask play

If you find yourself on the wild side of life, like me and many others, unbothered by all of these things listed above know you are not alone. Please Join me for my debut novel 'No Love Lost'.

Love,
  M

This one's for the girls who don't think there is anything more romantic than a man who cares enough to kidnap you.

You are totally fucking right.

1

Violet

I can feel the eyes on me.
The unanswered questions in the air.
The curiosity my classmates are horrible at trying to disguise as kindness.

Professor Ayla's sad stare and her eyes looming over me.

I take a deep breath, wrap up my presentation, and finish with, "Any questions?" Regret fills me immediately when we make eye contact.

"Yeah, what are you doing tonight, Violet? I know Vic's a little preoccupied." There are some shocked noises and a few quiet laughs from some of his douche friends.

Like he doesn't know the answer to that. It's not a secret my sister overdosed three weeks ago. The circumstances surrounding her apparent suicide have remained a bit fuzzy, but I know my twin would never have killed herself.

No, she wasn't the happiest person I'd ever met and she certainly didn't light up a room when she walked in. She made her fair share of enemies, but she was the realest person I knew. Victoria was so in tune with herself and the shitty world we lived in. She was dead set on making a difference in the world and she didn't care who she pissed off on her way there.

She only managed the dead part, so now I'll have to finish the rest.

Professor Ayla interrupts whatever trash was bound to come out of his mouth next.

"That will be enough, Mr. Endlow." I hear her speak from somewhere in the back of the room, but I keep my stare locked on him. This was the first time I was seeing him since Victoria's funeral. I stayed with my parents for a little over a week and then came straight to class this morning. I could tell by the look on his face that we'd be finishing this conversation later.

I know he wasn't involved in Victoria's death because he was with me that night. Brad will never let me forget that while my twin was suffocating on her own vomit I was doing shots of vodka, hanging off his arm.

I've wondered if I were a better sister maybe Vic would still be here, but it's an abhorrent thought. I can't change fate.

Thirty minutes pass in the miserably cold classroom. After were dismissed I race to the threshold of the door, hoping to beat him out of here, but something stops me dead in my tracks.

I feel it.

This paranoid feeling that's been following me for months. I scan my surroundings but there are only students moving from place to place, not a single person with their eyes solely focused on me.

The feeling has been there for a while now but the crippling sensation I have at this moment only started in the few weeks leading up to Victoria's death. I can't shake this constant inkling that I'm under observation.

Ultimately, I don't dig too deep because that's just it, I am.

My parents, Brad, and his parents.

They're all watching me.

Watching every move I make, every person I talk to, what I order from the coffee shop down the road.

To them my life's purpose is to maintain the image of the perfect senators daughter and soon to be housewife of the up and coming hotshot criminal defense attorney. I am nothing more than a pawn to a game I was never taught how to play.

I try and brush off the eerie sensation and continue on my way. I need to head to Economics but I just don't have it in me today. For a second I wonder if it's safer to stay here at school where I'm surrounded by people or throw a loop in my usually consistent routine. I go with the ladder and turn on my heel to head home.

"Not so fast, doll." The voice hits me like a vat of ice water dumped over my head. Brad snakes an arm around my waist. I try to recoil and protect myself with some distance but his fingernails dig in too deep.

I throw on a smile that doesn't quite reach my eyes. "Sorry, kind of in a hurry Brad."

Brad fucking Endlow. The bane of my existence and that's putting it lightly. I try not to let the bile rising up my throat fall out of my mouth and onto his freshly polished, dark dress shoes.

As kids we all got along great. Brad is just over two years older than Victoria and I and our parents have been friends since we were in diapers. We would swim in the pool at his house in the summer and his family would come to aspen with us in the winter.

As we got older our mom started drinking more and Vic's wild side started to rear its head. My dad nor Brad's could stand to have their reputations tarnished, so we stayed in and away from everyone.

While I've always been the peacemaker, Vic was the rebel. Where she was more than happy to stand up to our dad, I was doing my best trying to keep us all together. So on my 16th birthday when they randomly had the Endlow's over for dinner and told me that I belonged to Brad, I obliged.

I wasn't sure what would happen if they tried to pull a stunt like that on my twin so I accepted my fate willingly.

Victoria left that day and I didn't see her for two years until our 18th birthday. She'd surprised me on the last day of my senior year at the high school we once shared.

It was then that she let me know not only did she get her GED while hiding out with some other runaways, but she was going to be attending St. Lane University with me in the fall.

I feel sick when I think back to that day. I wish she would have stayed gone, maybe she'd still be alive.

"In a hurry? Where could you possibly be headed off to when you have another class in 25 minutes?" He was still smiling as his friends gazed at us from nearby but I could see the anger flash in his eyes. He's been more cautious about making a commotion in public, Daddy Endlow is tired of bailing his son out.

Theodore Endlow, Brad's father, is an infamous criminal defense lawyer. He's away more than he's home and when he is in Michigan I do my best to keep my distance. He's always been polite but he has a way of making you feel inferior that I try not to subject myself to unnecessarily.

I've become accustomed to the facade I'm forced to portray at all times. Not just during election season or when there's a big trial taking place. Brad, however, has some anger management issues that his toddler brain can't seem to work through. He's found himself on magazine covers and local newspapers a handful of times before his dad is able to do damage control. Mostly drunk driving and various other vehicular offenses but on occasion someone would capture him belittling a waitress or punching someone in the face for daring to look at him the wrong way.

"I'm not feeling great, I think I'm coming down with something." I will my face to pale in this exact fucking moment.

"Why do I feel like you're lying to me, Violet?" I know what it means when he lets my full name roll off his lips so smoothly.

I shut my eyes and think back to the last time Brad was this mad at me. We were arguing about something so insignificant that I can't recall at a dinner party a while back. Brad felt like I was defying him in front of his peers so he drug me by my hair out to his little sports car and smashed my face into the window repeatedly while he drove 125mph, drunk, down the wooded back roads.

It's not hard to piss the man off but apparently I have a knack for it. He only calls me by birth name when his anger has gotten the best of him and he's on the precipice of no return.

But I try to appeal to whatever sliver of sanity may be lurking inside him anyways.

"It's probably anxiety, I feel like everyone is watching me. I'm uncomfortable." I make sure not to mention Vic.

"Oh, I'm sorry." he says with obviously no sincerity. "You know what? I think I'll come with you, I've missed you and I can't have my fiancee home alone when she's not feeling well."

Well, I tried. I can sense the malice in his tone a mile away. We've only been apart for a little over a week and he's going to make me pay for every second of it.

"I'd love that." I reply sweetly, hoping for just an inch of forgiveness.

I know better.

2

Violet

Brad unlocks the front door to the house his parents bought us near campus. I was so excited to live in the dorms with Victoria our freshmen year, but my wonderful parents were able to "help" me evade the first year rule. Obviously with more space and independence in a house with my soon-to-be fiancee I'd surely be happier.

They know what "independence" looks like with Brad.

As I step through the antique oak doors, paranoid from earlier that someone may have followed us, I quickly turn to shut and lock them when my face and body are thrown up against the frosted glass. Straight away I can feel my cheek bone throb. "Do you think I'm fucking stupid, Violet?" Stupid? Debatable. Psychotic? Yes.

"No, Brad." I do my best lace my sarcastic tone with venom.

"Then why are you playing these games with me?" Spit flies onto the side of my face. "Did you think that would be it? You'd run back to mommy and daddy and I wouldn't say shit about it because your junkie sister killed herself?"

"How can I get it through your thick fucking skull that you're mine, Violet? You'll never be anything but MY fucking wife."

Honestly I should have considered the consequences when I left without saying goodbye after the funeral. I know better than to ignore his bountiful texts and constant phone calls, but I was hoping to find refuge in my childhood home. I was naive to think going from a family of four to to a family of three would bother the people who raised us.

There is no difference between having one daughter and two if you can only bargain one of them off.

I thought they'd understand I needed a few days away after my twin unexpectedly passed away. Apparently since they were hardly phased by the "ordeal", I shouldn't be either.

My dad didn't want me home longer than necessary. He was reluctant at first but eventually was able to talk Brad into giving us a little over a week for "family time."

I couldn't be bothered to feel anything even close to resembling gratitude.

"Whatever you say." I don't hide the indifference in my tone. I surely don't let on that he's hurting my shoulder because he'd get off on it and I can already feel him hardening against my back. At 6' 3" I don't stand a chance in a wrestling match, so I just comply. I stopped trying to fight back a long time ago.

"You've been bad, Violet." He spins me to face him and squeezes my face so hard that my mouth opens. "You know what happens to bad girls?" I hear him pull his zipper down with his other hand but I don't dare move my eyes away from his.

He pulls my face down hard leading me to my knees and gives the sore die of my face a light slap, "Answer me."

"They're punished." I grit out.

"Fuck." he adjusts himself. "You look like such a good little slut on your knees for me." Abruptly he pulls back and then plunges his cock deep into my throat while I try not to wince. I attempt to relax and brace myself for the next thrust.

I've learned to separate my mind from my body at times like this.

"Atta girl." He pumps faster, slamming into me over and over until I finally gag. I know he loves to hear it so I let go and give in. I gag over and over, drool falling down my chin. I'm beyond embarrassment at this point in our relationship. I would have to give a fuck what he thought about me to feel such a thing.

Unsatisfied with my lack of enthusiasm, he rips me up by my hair and leads me over to the couch where he takes a seat. "Now." Is all he says gesturing over to the table next to us. I know exactly what he means. On the coffee table there is a long, stained, flat piece of wood. To the naked eye it would look like a beautiful wooden center piece or maybe a fancy charcuterie board. It's not, it was a gift to Brad from his father. Theo told him that all women needed correction sometimes with a wink, passing the paddle over. I thought it was a joke or a sexual innuendo at the least but I clearly misjudged the level of cruelty that runs in the Endlow genes.

I hesitate for only a second before I grab the board and pass it over.

Brad rips the paddle from my hands and moves his arms out of the way as he waits for me to lay across his lap.

The only thing keeping this neat little bubble that we call our life afloat is my fake submission. He can use my body and believe the insincere words he forces from me all he wants. I'm only biding my time until I learn the truth about my sister and then I'll be gone.

For now, I float away into the abyss that is my subconscious and slightly register him shift behind me.

He shoves me down further and I feel something sharp graze my thigh while he rips my leggings and thong down.

"I've missed this ass." He gives my left cheek a squeeze and a stinging bite making me jump. "Move again Violet, I fucking dare you."

I try to go back to that place in my head but some days are more difficult than others when I'm this overstimulated. The energy in the air is buzzing and I barely have time to note the movement coming behind me.

WHACK!

"Ten hits for ten days away."

WHACK!

I can feel tears welling in my eyes. I don't know if its from the pain of the wooden board I'm being struck with or the grief that's suddenly flooding my system.

"Brad I'm sorry, I'm sor-"

WHACK!

WHACK!

I haven't cried yet.

I haven't shed a single tear since I found my sister face down in some random upstairs bedroom. The tears are flowing now. They're so hot on my skin, the trail they leave behind burns.

My only sibling is gone. My twin. My best friend.

My only friend.

"Beg me not to hit you again. Beg me not to mark your pale skin my favorite shade of red."

In a moment of weakness I believe that Brad might show me some mercy.

"Please Brad. I'm sorry!"

WHACK!

I don't make a sound while I anticipate what's to come.

Sure enough Brad doesn't hesitate before swinging the board down the final five times at full force. I hate myself for sobbing now while Brad's cock twitches beneath my stomach.

"You're so beautiful when you cry." He strokes the hair on the back of my head gently. "We should do this more often."

He shimmies out from under me laying my top half down on the couch and throws a pillow under my hips, tilting my ass up to him.

He thrusts in deep with no warning or lubrication. I try and lean into the darkness in my head and allow myself to drift somewhere else but I can't. The intensity were engulfed in is too high and I don't do well with emotions.

He lifts up on my wrists causing a shooting pain down both shoulders. I let out an involuntary shriek and he drills into me harder. All I feel is pain. There is no pleasure to chase in this void that is my life. With my arms at this angle I'm sure they're going to fucking snap.

I try my best to act unbothered by the relentless pain in my lower stomach and shoulders until I finally feel him jerking inside of me. He gives my sore ass a hard slap and I feel his hand slide down my back to the back of my neck and then around my throat. He lowers his heavy body down on top of me, nearly cutting off my airway completely. His mouth is right up against my ear and I can feel his breath.

"Maybe next semester a Communications course would be more valuable." He gives me a small thrust shoving the cum seeping out of me back inside.

"It seems your skills have gotten rusty and you've found yourself in a pretty shitty predicament." I can feel him grin against my neck.

"A dead twin and a sore ass. Sad stuff."

I try to turn my head away and he gives my neck a squeeze bringing my eyes to his.

"Tell me you won't runoff like that again, Violet."

I say nothing. The submissiveness eludes me.

"SAY IT VIOLET!" His hand meets my face with a loud crack.

"Fuck Brad, I won't run off!" I yell back in his face trying to pull back but his grip on my throat is unabating.

With that he pushes up and out of me leaving me naked from the waste down on the couch.

"Get the fuck out of my sight."

I stand up and grab my leggings but they're in shreds. I cover myself as best I can and head up the stairs to my favorite place.

As soon as I reach the bathroom I shut the door and lock it. It's only a simple twist lock but I need the false sense of security, just for a moment.

This bathroom is my only haven. When we moved into this house the only upstairs bathroom was connected to the master and Brad decided he didn't want my "girl shit" in his way. So I was able to have this one built and design it myself. The floors are a heated white tile that sparkle in the sunlight. The natural lighting meets every corner and crevice from the skylights. Off to the right is the smaller sink basin and toilet but to the left is my vanity. A huge quartz counter on bamboo with ring lighting and an expanse of drawers. One side containing makeup and hair supplies the other contains all my bath and shower favorites.

I pull open the drawer full of my extensive bath supplies and see a small, folded piece of paper sitting on my new bath salts.

I know it wasn't there when I left for my parents last week. Brad doesn't use my bathroom but I'm sure he would have looked in here while I was MIA.

I flip it over and my brows draw in. All the dark ideas I had festering float away when I read the words written in dark ink.

See you soon, *Mio Angelo*

3

Violet

After my bath I personally make sure to dispose of the note I'd found in the drawer. I light it up and let it fly out the window, watching the pieces disintegrate as the wind sweeps them away.

Running through a mental list of suspects, the earlier feeling that I was being watched creeps in but I quickly let it pass. If I was unable to do a single thing outside of Brad's watchful eye, how could someone else possibly slip through? They couldn't, it was that simple.

After that, I don't put a lot of thought into the origin of the anonymous letter, probably some sick game Brad wants to play. I toss around the idea of mentioning it to him, but ultimately decided against it just in case.

It's only been three weeks since Victoria left me here to fend for myself, and I'd never felt more lost. For three weeks I'd gone over the events of that day and night over and over until I couldn't think straight. Nothing was out of the ordinary. We went to class, we got dressed up, we partied.

Only this time when Brad told me it was time to go, I couldn't find Vic to tell her goodbye.

I knew.

I knew immediately that something was off. Not only was it off, it was gone.

She was gone.

There was one thing odd about the night. Victoria told me we needed to talk. She said it was nothing major but it needed to be done in private. AKA, away from Brad. She didn't trust my fiancee as far as she could throw him. I don't blame her, neither did I.

We never did get to have that conversation and its been eating at me ever since. While I was no medium, I knew one way to communicate with the dead.

Find her cell phone.

I let out a sigh of relief when I realize I'm alone upon opening my eyes. While sleeping next to my beloved tormentor I'm usually as rested and recharged as one would expect.

I get out of bed and push along with my typical morning routine. I brush my teeth, throw my hair up in a loose bun, and put on a little mascara and blush.

I do my best to find an outfit that would be deemed appropriate by Brad for school. I grab a quick change of clothes and throw them in my bag for later.

As I come down the stairs I make sure to put on a satisfactory smile and propel a little bit of authenticity into my movements.

I have plans today to meet up with an old classmate from high school who happens to be in my biology class now. She was really more Victoria's friend than mine but I have no intention of befriending her further.

I'm only using her. I know it sounds bad but I have work to do.

When Kellan's cousin went missing a few years ago I discovered that her uncle was a police officer in the next town over. I need to speak to him and I'm hoping she can be my in.

I can't go to our police station, they are all considerably close to the Endlow family and of course my father. I can't escape the influence of my family or his here, so I'd have to venture out.

"Good morning", I speak a little too dryly coming down the stairs.

"What's the point in keeping you around if I'm down here making my own coffee?" The malevolence in his tone palpable. There is no escaping our relationship for either of us, our fathers simply would not allow it.

Either way, I really had to hold in my eye roll if I wanted to make it out of here on time today. "Sorry, I must not have heard my alarm the first time this morning. I'm still feeling a little off."

"Lazy like your fucking mom. I wish people saw the side of you that I see. I'd love to be a woman today and not have to do a fucking thing." It's not unlike Brad to talk shit about my family. He's hated Victoria since she protested our arranged relationship two years ago and he belittles my moms alcoholism any chance he gets hoping to hit a nerve down deep somewhere.

"Could you imagine if I just told the firm 'Sorry I didn't show up guys, my alarm clock didn't go off'" Like I gave a fuck whether he shows up to his job at his fathers law firm. I'm pretty sure his dad just pays him to show up and not cause any problems at this point.

VIOLET

He's not a lawyer or anything yet, I couldn't even tell you what he does there. Though, he loves to hold it over my head that he'll be the best criminal defense attorney this country has ever seen. Some how I doubt that but I keep it to myself.

I throw an arm around his waist and happily oblige him, "You're right babe, it won't happen again." I let a grin paint itself across my face. No matter the bullshit I'm spewing, I will leave this house today and I refuse to come back empty handed.

Miraculously, I manage to make it out of the house unscathed. Now I just have to find somewhere to change and locate my lunch date.

"Violet!" The loud shriek pulls me from my thoughts, perfect timing. I turn to see Kellan's bright white smile and purple hair headed straight toward me.

"Kellan! Hey! Are you ready?" I smile, paranoid her loud voice will attract too much attention.

As much as I don't enjoy the high-pitched, giddy tone it's kind of nice to talk to someone else. It's been a solid three weeks since I've interacted with anyone other than Brad and my parents. Even longer if you exclude Victoria.

"Yes, starving. What are you in the mood for? Thai? Italian?" She rattles off, what seems like one hundred places, easily.

It's always interesting to watch people with genuine happiness. I can spot authentic emotion a mile away, it was a talent that I'm pretty sure has kept me alive a time or two.

I don't know if it's because of my cold, hollow innards but I can always sense a genuine heat or lack thereof in others emotions. I've been shoving down any inclination of emotion for so long now that my receptors are shot.

I felt pain when I lost Victoria, I feel anger when I think about the dismissal I received when I tried to go to the police, and I feel a strong dislike toward the man I unfortunately share a life with.

Even with all that said, the severity at which I feel those things could almost be leveled with indifference. The emotions always try to wash over but they cant. They come and then they go.

If I sat around and collected feelings for all the things that have pissed me off or made me upset I'd end up 6 feet under with my twin.

She'd be pissed about that.

So right now, I'll focus on my newest hobby.

Finding out what the fuck happened to my sister.

I muster up best schoolgirl attitude I've got, "Oooh, how about Thai? I haven't been to the place around the corner in forever!"

"Deal!" Kellan shouts and then hooks her elbow in mine.

I look around one last time making sure Brad hasn't heard or seen us when I see a man I've never seen before with his eyes locked on me.

I'm temporarily blinded by his deep brown wavy hair bristling a bit in the wind and his blinding smile. I've got to be at least fifty yards from the guy and his beauty is apparent from here.

He winks and turns for the administration building parking lot. Between his quick movements and the people passing by, he's out of sight before I so much as blink.

4

Violet

"So, Violet, how have you been? It's been so long!" Kellan asks radiating sunshine.

She's a smart girl, I know she's probably wondering why I wanted to meet up with her after not having talked in a few years.

When my parents handed me over to Brad my life changed drastically, in every way. I no longer have time for friends. If I'm not studying I'm playing pretend at a charity event or volunteering to make my fiancee seem like a better person.

I don't subscribe to this shit but going with the flow has always proven to be easier. I've come to terms with the fact that I will soon be in a loveless marriage, bound to a man who is so obsessed with my ownership that I have no time allotted to build any platonic relationships. Regardless, I'm sure that whole sentiment would ruin the mood.

So, I lie.

"I know! I'm sorry, things have just been so crazy with wedding planing and Vic, of course" She lets out small sigh and frowns. I knew that would get her. "I just needed some girl time and you were the first person I thought of."

"Of course! I'm so glad you reached out, I've missed you both." She plays with her hands a little as we sit and wait for the waiter to come back with our drinks. People typically have a hard time looking me in the eye when we talk about Victoria, I expect it now.

"We'll have to make this more of a habit then." I tell her with a wide smile, knowing I have no intention of doing so. I'll be lucky if this doesn't get back to Brad, let alone a second attempt. "How's your family been?"

"Pretty good, they moved to Florida to avoid the seasons and I miss them, but they're good." I can tell she's unhappy to be alone. Kellan's family is small and she was close to her cousin, Samantha, before she went missing. Samantha was only in the grade ahead of us attending St. Lane's when she left for class one day and never made it back. Her backpack was found on the sidewalk in broad daylight but no evidence could be collected and she was never seen again.

After some mundane conversation about family and school I move forward with phase two of my plan. I have to remind myself to be extra sensitive with Kellan, she hasn't been conditioned not to feel that way I have.

"Kell, I did want to talk to you about something today." I trail off a bit. "I know it's hard but Vic's passing has made me think of all types of things recently and.. I was just wondering if maybe I could speak to your uncle? Samanthas dad?"

Her face goes red and she doesn't speak for a minute as she stares at her hands "We can't get ahold of him."

Fuck. "Is he still working? Surely someone has tried to call the station?" I can feel myself becoming a little more demanding, I try to tone it back a bit. I relax my shoulders and take a deep

VIOLET

breath.

"We have but they haven't seen him either, he hasn't been to work in months. I think that's why my parents left Violet, they can't handle anymore loss here." Kellan breaks down, tears streaming down her face. This is not what I signed up for today. Knowing that I can't speak to her uncle, I'm tempted to just get up and leave anyways.

"I'm sorry Kellan, I'll see if there is anything my dad do to help." Everyone knows that between my dad and Brad's, they've got more pull than the damn president himself.

"You'd do that? He's like a second father to me, Violet. I don't know how our family can stay together with out him and Samantha." I want to tell her they won't.

It'll all fall apart right before her eyes, like it has to me. I leave that out though, deciding I've already spent to much time here and I can't risk more tears. Out of nowhere the hairs on the back of my neck start to prickle.

"Of course! We should get going if we want to make it back in time to beat the after-lunch rush." With that we stand, hug briefly, and head our separate ways.

I can feel it again, I know I'm being watched. This trip was for absolutely nothing and now I've been caught by Brad.

I turn and walk as fast as I can without looking like I"m running from something, someone. I'd really hate for this punishment to be doubled because I was, again, "making a scene" in public.

I stay in highly populated areas while I race back to campus. I decide to take a back alley between two campus halls so I can slide into my sociology class without anyone noticing my arrival.

I realize my mistake when it's too late. I go to pull the hands off but the grip is unrelenting. There's a leather glove covering my mouth and another squeezing my throat with just enough pressure to make me question my sanity when I feel a familiar warmth growing deep in my belly.

Those thoughts come to an abrupt stop when I internally question the gloves. I shake my face away to try and speak to my attacker.

"Leather gloves, Brad? And a back alley on campus? This is weird, even for you."

My grave error is apparent when I hear a low chuckle and a deep, hoarse voice whisper in my ear, "Call me by another mans name, *Mio Angelo,* and you won't like the consequences."

I freeze. I'm certain I've only been called "my angel" in Italian one other time.

Before I can respond to the random fucking man holding my body up against his in a back alley, I feel a sharp prick in my neck. I throw my hand up to my neck in surprise, almost expecting to feel a goddamn nail sticking out.

Turning a little slower than normal to spout my usual sarcastic bullshit at him I realize I can't. My lips are heavy and won't move. My eyes are starting to close and I'm not sure if its seconds, minutes, or hours that pass before I feel him gently lift my feet off the ground and hold me close to him bridal style.

Eventually I feel his hand smooth my hair down and his lips on the back of my head. He whispers something ineligible close to my face. I try to scream in response but my muscles refuse to cooperate.

And then I'm asleep.

5

Vincenzo

I wasn't expecting to take violet today, I was hoping I could just follow her back to her class. That was until I checked the tracking app on Brad's phone and saw him headed toward her. I'm sure one of his friends tipped him off when they saw Violet leave the school grounds.

Now unfortunately for me I'm stuck rushing things and I am not a spontaneous man. My life is meticulously planned down to each minute of the day. Spontaneous men in my line of work don't live for long.

I monitor all of my clients locations. Occasionally there incoming and outgoing communications as well. Sometimes for weeks, months, years. As long as I need to be certain they will stay a client rather than an unassuming victim.

I trust no one, I can't.

That idiot was going to hurt my angel and I decided today was the last day they'd be in contact. Violet is strong but I can see that she's near her breaking point. Physically and mentally. My girl needs an impromptu vacation, she can be spontaneous for the both of us.

I will make sure he pays for his role in tarnishing Violet's life, but not until I'm able to use him to my advantage. In the mean time sit tight and enjoy my time with her until I can end his life.

When I took Brad Endlow on as a client I was thrilled to find what I'd unearth.

His dad is a smart man and covers his tracks well. Fortunately for me his son is reckless. Theodore has evaded any type of authority or public scrutiny for years. I know just as well as any other Joe in this city that they're bad people.

What they don't know is that I'm after them. And I'm worse. Much, much worse.

So, for a while I let Brad think I was working for him. Hiring a hit out on his soon to be sister in law purely out of jealousy and spite was cutthroat, even for me.

At first I even considered killing Victoria myself to keep our rapport intact, but someone else beat me to it and cut my contract short.

Violet was only collateral. A precious insurance policy that I knew I wouldn't be able to keep my hands off of. At some point along the way the pull I felt for her became all consuming.

I'm obsessed.

The irresistible girl in my lap starts to stir.

I stroke her long golden blonde hair draped across my lap. I've been watching her sleep the last few hours. My angel doesn't really dabble in drugs like her sister so the sedative hit her hard.

I watch her eyelids flutter until the silver irises are fully exposed. "Good morning, *Bella Ragazza*"

She rubs her eyes and then jumps up but I can tell the

movement causes her head to throb when she winces. I can't hold in my chuckle. She's like a startled bunny and it's adorable.

"Who the fuck are you?" She insists.

"Sit down Violet and we'll talk." My tone's stern but she doesn't listen. She continues to back up toward the door. "How do you know my name?"

"I know everything about you, Vi." She wrinkles her brow a bit. "I know you hate the color yellow. I know you had your tonsils taken out when you were 8. I know your favorite number is 13. I know your mom is a drunk. I know your dad is a serial adulterer. And I know that your sister was your only friend up until her death." I could continue, the list goes on. I truly don't think there is anything she could tell me that I haven't learned from research or watching her for the last 6 months.

"Now, sit the fuck down."

She hesitates and then walks back toward the couch, sitting as far from me as she can.

I can't help but smile, the three feet in between us will do absolutely nothing to save her from me. There is nothing that could.

"Thank you. What would you like to know?"

"What would I like to know? Are you fucking serious?" I don't love the tone of voice she's using with me but I let her rant for a moment. "Hm, let's start with why I'm here? Or maybe why you felt compelled to drug me? Better yet, WHO THE FUCK ARE YOU?"

She's raising her voice now. I can almost smell the fear radiating off of her and its making me hard. I adjust myself in my pants and stand up.

"Since you asked so kindly, I'm Vincenzo Bianchi. And you, Violet Elaine Woodruff, are my newest item of infatuation."

Her shudder is visible as I watch her pupils dilate. This is the biggest reaction I've seen out of her since I started Brad's job. My reputation precedes me and my angel knows who I am.

"Vincenzo Bianchi, like the hit man? The guy on the news?" She's shaking a little and fuck if I don't want to slide her skirt up and see if she's feeling what I'm feeling right now.

I don't respond and she starts to ramble.

"Why would anyone have a hit out on me? Is this about Victoria? Did you kill her?"

"Slow down little one. I'm not going to hurt you, not in anyway that you won't like at least." I give her a wink and she blushes.

She rubs her thighs together and I'm pretty sure my cock is going to bust through the seam of my jeans.

"And no, I did not kill Victoria. Hit man is a strong word, didn't Brad tell you that in this country we are all innocent until proven otherwise?"

I can't tell her what I know about Victoria right now. She doesn't trust me yet. There are some walls to break down, but I have time. Luckily for me the only person in Violets life who showed her even an ounce of love was murdered a few weeks ago so I don't have much competition.

Once I show my sweet girl how she deserves to be treated we can fulfill my little project and I can wash my hands of these people once and for all.

"You won't fucking touch me, you psycho."

"Please don't challenge me Violet, I don't make bets I won't win." I smirk and I can tell she's already relaxing a bit when she rolls her eyes at me in return.

"I promise not to touch you without your permission, okay?" When she doesn't respond I widen my eyes signifying that I'm looking for a response.

"Okay." She says it a little louder than she means and shifts uncomfortably.

"Good girl." We're going to have so much fun together.

I start toward the door to leave but she stops me.

"Why did you take me today, Vince? I don't understand."

"Because the first time I saw you, Violet, I knew you were meant for me. I won't stand by and share what's mine with another man." The tension is so thick I'm afraid it might snap.

"The house is staffed 24/7, if you need anything please pick up the phone and Noelle will assist you. The door to the left is the closet and the right is the bathroom." With that said I walk out and shut the door. I don't want to lock it behind me but its too soon, I can't trust her not to leave right now.

Now, I'm in my office in the opposite wing of the castle watching her explore her room. Her accommodations are far from modest and while her parents are wealthy it's nothing compared to the income of the best hit man this century has seen.

I work for no one, I have the Russian and Italian mafia's in my pocket, along with the FBI, and most of the political officials on all seven continents. I work globally and have yet to be prosecuted for as much as a parking ticket. However, the media loves to follow me.

So I bought a small island under a fake business name between Michigan and Canada in Lake Huron. I built my castle here roughly 9 years ago when the feds were a little too close for comfort.

It turns out it only takes one dirty agent to rid yourself of a pesky homicide investigation. In return I now live in a beautiful stone castle surrounded by nothing but family and water, only reachable by private aircraft or boat.

Win-win if you ask me.

Violet is roaming the walk-in closet right now. I wonder what she thinks about all of the items it's already been stocked with? I doubt she'd guess I'd had them all brought here for her, let alone notice they're her exact size and style.

I watch her as she walks back to the bed and notices the blanket I grabbed from her house before I took her this morning. Immediately she brings it up to her face, no doubt checking it's actually hers and not a duplicate. She takes her jean jacket off and lays down on the bed.

I take that as my invitation to take my aching cock out.

I use the bead of precum at the tip and stroke myself gently at first and then build up speed. I close my eyes and think about long blonde hair wrapped around my fist while I pump my thick cock in and out of the her warm mouth.

I can't wait to see those piercing grey eyes stare into my soul with my dick deep in her throat. The thought alone is almost enough to make me bust.

Just then I open my eyes to take a good look at my captive and she's taking her leather skirt off to trade for a pair of shorts she must of found in the closet. I beat my dick violently and thick white lines of come flow out of me and onto my stomach.

I haven't had to jack off since I was a prepubescent boy and I don't plan to do it again. After I laid eyes on Violet I couldn't touch anyone else. For 6 months I've been jerking off into a pair of panties I stole from her room. But, she's here now and luckily I can rid myself of the habit and start a new one.

VINCENZO

I'll give her a few days to adjust but from here on out I internally vow that Violet and I will be exchanging all orgasms.

6

Violet

Basically what I heard was the guy has stalked me for a few months and now he thinks were soulmates.

Great, he's literally psychotic. I can tell there will be absolutely no reasoning with him at this point.

I run my hand over the racks of clothing in the walk-in closet. There are so many different textures, the small materialistic part of me ogles all the designer brands. The clothes are different shades of black or jewel toned. If I didn't know any better I would have thought I was in my own closet back home before I moved in with Brad. I was almost immediately forced to wear the bright colors he thought his soon-to-be wife should be seen in.

I push thoughts of the other psycho plaguing my life out of my head quickly as I sit on the bench near the shoes. I wonder what poor woman sat here before me. No doubt drugged and kidnapped the way I was.

I am just now realizing that I am royally fucked.

Even if I was able to get through one of the windows in the room I'm not sure how I'd make the drop down. I've got to be at least 2 stories up, if not more. There is nothing on the wall of the building to attempt to hold onto and scale down.

   I pull open a drawer and its full of lace. Lace bras, panties, and other lingerie. I quickly shut it and move to the next. Here I find more suitable pajama type items. I grab a pair of cotton shorts and leave the closet.

   I make my way back to the bed when I spot something familiar. I feel a flicker in my heart when I notice my most prized comfort item draped perfectly across the bed. I bring the fabric to my nose and take a deep breath in. It's definitely my blanket and not an imposter. I smell the faint cherry blossom from the fabric softener I use and warm vanilla from my body wash and spray. I should probably find it weird that my kidnapper thought to bring my childhood blanket with him when he abducted me but I only notice the fuzzy feeling registering somewhere deep that someone cared enough to do so.

   I slide my skirt down and pull the shorts up. My crop top is comfy enough to wear with the shorts to sleep in. While I'm finishing up that intrusive sensation I'm being watched returns. I glance around the room quickly, once I don't see anything I dive under the blankets pulling mine over top of my neck and shoulders.

   I'm not sure how long I was out or what time it is now but I can see that its dark outside. When I look out the windows on the far side of the room there is only water. Has he taken to me to the ocean? It would take at least twelve hours to get to the nearest part of the ocean. That timing doesn't really work out, maybe its a lake or large river? Plus the trees outside the window near the bed looks like the trees at home. They are tall and covered with different shades of red and orange leaves, some are pines that I thought I caught a faint whiff of upon waking up earlier.

I stop pondering my whereabouts as sleep overwhelms me. Im not sure how I'm able to close my eyes and drift off at a time like this. But I can, and I do.

I feel the sun on my face as I slowly open my eyes. I rise from the bed and make my way over to the windows. I stare ahead at the body of water in front of me and stretch my back. I haven't slept that good in years. Maybe even a decade. Sleep has evaded me since I was old enough to wake up when my mom came home from her drunken escapades. I would hold her hair back and make sure she didn't choke on her own vomit. She wasn't the best mom but I'm not sure Victoria and I would have survived our father without her.

I wasn't surprised when my father told me I would be marrying Brad when I turned twenty one. Or that he still felt comfortable back handing me at 16 years old whenever I told him no. Even when brad showed up that night and took me against my will while I pleaded with him not too, it wasn't shocking to see him sit back relaxed like we weren't screaming at one another. I was, however, surprised that my mom sat idly by while this went on, while Victoria trashed our living room and left that night, and while I was robbed of what little innocence I had left.

That fateful night had led me to my nihilistic attitude. I had no urge to keep my family together any longer. I was done with optimism. There was no one to help me then and there is no one to help me now.

On that positive note, I lift myself from the bed and walk to the bathroom. My mouth tastes horrible, I desperately need to brush my teeth. To my surprise when I open the door there's an unopened tooth brush on the counter and my favorite brand of toothpaste next to it.

I decide to spend some more time snooping around the gorgeous room. The floors and counter top are black marble. There's a double sink and a toilet separated by a wall on the other side. What really catches my eye is the walk in shower. It's the same beautiful black with matte black shower heads, one connected to each wall and one directly in the center. There are switches and gauges on the wall near the entrance, I look at the small pictures on the panel and discover they change the lighting, sounds, and flow of the water.

Stepping back out I begin opening all the drawers. The top left drawer holds some beauty products, make up wipes, cotton balls, etc. The one beneath holds some similar items that I use at home for my hair. I go for a black scrunchie and throw my hair into a messy bun on top of my head not worried about impressing the psycho that has me trapped here.

I move to the top right drawer and am caught off guard by my.. birth control? It's on yesterdays pill just as it should be. I had this hidden at home. No one, especially not Brad, new I was taking birth control. My strict catholic parents never would have allowed it. My marriage to Brad and any children with him were a golden ticket tying my family to the Endlow's for eternity, something my father seemed to be desperate for.

Between the other items in the bathroom, the clothes in the closet, and my blanket I'm starting to wonder if it's all coincidental or Vince really does know everything about me. I mean even the bras in the drawer were the correct size.

I brush my teeth and splash some water on my face when a thought slaps me in the face. While I was fantasizing throwing myself out of the window and onto the cement below, I realize never actually tried the door handle last night. I finish up in the bathroom and scurry over to the door. I give it a twist and much to my dismay, it's locked.

Shrugging it off, I look over at the extensive book shelf near the couch Vince and I sat on last night and decide I will spend my day reading. I never had time to read for pleasure at home. I just reached the shelf, but before I could grab what I assumed from the cover was something spicy, the bolt on the door shifts and it swings open.

Vince walks through with a smug grin like he owns the place. I mean, he does but right now this is my room. And he has no reason to be smirking like that. His dark brown hair hangs into his face a little but is tightly tapered on the sides. You would think his hair was black in this lighting but I know its not. I know now he was the beautiful man with the chocolatey hair staring at me on campus just a day ago. I can tell he's been up for a while, maybe all night. His emerald eyes are rimmed a dark red. His looks are shockingly beautiful. A complete contrast to Brad's straight blonde hair and blue eyes.

Brad isn't a small guy by any means, but Vince has got at least three inches on him. Brad works out and is well defined but Vince is broad and sturdy. Brad's skin is pale and unmarked, where Vince is olive toned with tattoos running from his fingertips up his biceps and under his shirt. If only. I wasn't his captive I would wonder where they end, but I don't of course. That would be inappropriate. Right? Vince has got to be in his late twenties or early thirties. I know I've seen him in the news since I started watching it with the nanny in middle school.

"Good morning, *Mio Angelo*." he purrs at me like this has been our morning routine for years.

I roll my eyes and turn back around to grab the book that caught my eyes just moments ago.

"Oh my angel, if you keep acting like a brat I'll be forced to treat you as such." His voice is deep and thick like honey. I want to hear him say something dirtier, darker, quieter for just me to hear.

I'm so fucked.

"I'm sorry, my skills as a captive are a bit rusty. I'll try to be more receptive." I don't bother turning around as I speak. I reach for the book as I'm abruptly spun around and my hips are pushed up against his.

"I would hardly call you my captive, love. I doubt captives are accommodated with king sized beds and jacuzzi tubs."

"I don't think your accommodations negate the fact that I have been kidnapped and brought to your cave against my will, dickhead." I toss out with a blatantly fake smile. I don't care to play nice with this guy. He's either going to get use to me the way I am or he can kill me.

More power to you, buddy.

He lets out a roar of laughter and while unexpected I can't say I hate the sound. I keep my composure, refusing to show him anymore emotion. Not fear, not sadness, not lust, nothing. I don't give it to others and I sure as fuck won't give it to him. I gave the rest of my tears and sadness to Victoria, my hatred to Brad, disgust to my parents. Vince will get nothing, not a single piece of my poor dilapidated soul.

Vince whips my head to the side with a tight grip around my neck and whispers in my ear, "You will be so fun to tame, *Bellisima.*"

I can't do anything to stop him when he bites down hard enough on my ear lobe that I shriek and then sucks it into his mouth soothing the pain. There's also nothing I can do to stop the charged intensity bolting straight to my traitorous pussy forcing a moan out of me.

Her and I will be having words later, assuming I survive the until then.

7

Vincenzo

I storm toward the door and lock it on my way out again. I have no reason to be mad other than the fact that I made her moan in my fucking ear. I promised her I wouldn't touch her unless she begged me. I meant verbally not with her fucking eyes and here I am giving in and it hasn't even been twenty-four hours.

I lean my back against the door and take a deep breath. At least I have some work to do today so I have something else to think about besides the luscious lips and tits locked away in a room under my roof.

I walk past the kitchen and let Noelle know Violet is ready for her breakfast. It's almost lunch time but I know it's my angels favorite meal of the day, so I don't want her to miss out.

The first thing I do when I get to my office is pull up the camera feed from her room. She's in the reading chair I bought just for her with her feet kicked up reading some smut I strategically placed toward the front of the shelf.

I know my girl has a taste for dark romance and I plan to deliver that to her in more ways than one. I noticed the way she looked at me this morning, so for now I'll let her conjure up some ideas of her own and let her suffer the way I am.

I boot up my desk top computer and start tracking my newest victim. A man from Thailand who, unfortunately for him, pissed off the wrong people. Fortunately for me he's not as smart as he thinks he is. I was able to find him in only a few short hours using the bank account he had some money rerouted to. It's amusing he thought using a fake name would be enough to deter someone looking for a missing ten million dollars.

It was simple enough to track the number of ten million dollar bank transfers to off shore accounts on any given day, as you can imagine there aren't typically many. After some more digging I figure out that my friend here is hiding out in a small town in Costa Rica.

Bingo.

I hate to leave Violet but duty calls.

It takes me a few hours to pinpoint his exact location but eventually, I do. When I'm done I slide over to the camera feed in her room. I can't say I'm all that astounded that she hasn't touched her tray yet although I was hoping her favorite foods made fresh by my illustrious chef would be enticing enough.

She hasn't eaten since she's arrived to the island yesterday and I can't have her losing any of those curves I'm dying to trace with my hands and mouth. I make my way over to the wing of the house she's in and don't bother knocking when I enter.

"Eat, *Mio Angelo*." I'm being stern but to be honest I'm not in the mood to fuck around. Her attitude, as tempting as it may be, is a waste of my time and I need to get going. I can't afford to be distracted on a mission like this.

"No." She doesn't look at me when she speaks and its quickly wearing on my nerves.

"You'll eat or I'll make you. Your choice." It's taking everything in me not to reach out, grab her face and force her to face me. "Take it while you can, Violet. I'm not a man known to offer options."

With that she stands, stepping up to me with not more than an inch between us. I've got nearly a foot and a hundred pounds on her but you'd never be able to tell the way she just approached me. I can feel the heat simmering between our bodies as she stares me in the eye.

"I'm not hungry. I don't have to eat. I don't have to play your games. I'm going to finish reading my book and you are going to fuck off right on out of this stupid room." That does it.

Before I have time to think I'm grabbing the back of her neck and spinning her to press up against the wall next to the bookshelf. The uneaten food and book clattering to the ground behind us.

"I think you need to be shown whose in charge on this island, Vi." I wonder if she's accepting of the nickname coming from me, I've only ever heard her twin use it with her.

She doesn't speak.

She's breathing heavily and I can't help but to let my dick do the thinking right now. I slide my leg between her parted thighs and push up roughly against her clit. Her eyes roll back and a whimper leaves her plump lips.

"You know what else I think? I think you'd like me to show you. If I didn't know any better I'd think you just moaned for me again with your needy pussy pressed up against my leg." She tries to shake her head telling me no but I tighten my grip so she's unable.

I slide my free hand over her thick thigh. The skin is so

smooth, begging to be bitten and licked. I grab her where her leg connects to her hip and slide her back against my crotch and then down toward the wall. She moans again and I feel her shift her hips herself.

"Good girl, Violet. Ride my thigh." She shifts again running her hips back and forth again. She presses her clit down hard. I slide my hand from the base of her neck around to her jaw. Leaning in I suck and bite at her neck provoking her. She throws her head back inviting me in for more.

Soft moans and whimpers leave her lips grounding me into the moment. I move down to bite at her collarbone before sucking the same spot into my mouth.

I can tell she's close when she starts to pick up the pace. I use my hand on her hip to push her so she's flush up against the wall, unable to move.

"What the fuck?" She gasps. She's panting, trying to catch her breath. Her eyes search my face looking for a reason as to why I've put an abrupt stop to her orgasm.

"Ask me, Violet. Beg me." I can't help but think how close I am to watching her beautiful face explode into pure bliss. I use the grasp on her hip to restart the movement she was so thoroughly enjoying.

She lets out an exasperated noise and closes her eyes for a moment, letting her head fall forward against the wall.

"Please." She's so quiet I barley register the words.

"Please what, Violet?" I grind her down harder on my leg.

"Please let me come Vince." With that she turns a bit so her mouth can meet mine. It's an awkward angle but I pull her into me and let her explore my mouth with her tongue. I can feel the wet spot spreading over my jeans as she rocks her hips.

I suck her tongue into my mouth and moments later she's

exploding. I pull my head back and nibble on her bottom lip. She rubs her pussy on me a few more times, slow but hard before she comes to a complete stop and rests back against me.

I give her just a second to catch her breath before I decide I've enough and throw her up and over my shoulder, stalking over to the bed.

"Vince put me down. NOW!" She's so cute when she tries to raise her voice. She's telling me to stop but there is no heat in her tone, almost like she's saying it out of obligation.

"Yes ma'am." I stifle a laugh as I throw her down onto the bed and she lets out some air.

"That's not what I meant." There she goes again rolling those eyes. I let it slide this time because I noticed a glitter to them I haven't seen since I saw her six months prior.

She slides under the cream duvet and I cover only the top of her body with her blanket, just the way she likes it. She looks up at me with her brows furrowed a bit.

"What's the point of kidnapping someone to treat them like this?" I know she has questions, but I'm not in the mood to answer them yet. "I mean you brought or bought all of my favorite make up and hair items, you know my size, you brought my blanket. I just don't get it. It seems you aren't in the business of torture, what do you want from me?"

"Don't mistake my generosity and ability to plan things thoroughly for kindness, Violet. I have an agenda to fulfill just like the rest of the sick bastards you and I know." I don't mean to come off so harsh but I need her to know that while I thoroughly enjoy having her here with me, there's a bottom line. I'm going to end those who made her life miserable and in turn she will help me avenge Sofia, she just isn't aware of either of those things yet and I haven't decided how long I'll keep her in the dark yet.

She almost looks slightly hurt by my words but if she is she only lets it show for a quarter of a second.

"Noted." She rolls over to face away from me.

I head back to the book shelf and grab the book that fell during our heated moment. I toss it to her.

"I'll be gone for a few days but whatever you need, Noelle will be of service." I start toward the door. "I'm going to have her send another tray. Hopefully you can find your appetite this time." I can't help myself when I turn to take one last glance toward the beautifully flushed goddess laying in the center of the king-sized bed.

She's looking right back at me.

"Bye Vince, I hope nothing bad happens to you on your trip." She winks and rolls back over, opening her book.

With that I let out a full blown laugh.

Fuck, I like her.

8

Violet

Well, that didn't go as I'd planned. You've got to be seriously deranged to ask the psychotic man that kidnapped you to let you dry hump your little heart out on his leg.

I'm trying to continue with the book I found but the male main character is a blonde, clean-cut golden retriever and it's just not doing it for me. As much as I think the mental stability would be a nice change, I am regrettably damaged and can't imagine a man like that whispering sweet-nothings in my ear without cringing.

I was going to try and nap in the afterglow I was feeling from that mess but my mind is still racing so I ended up staring at the ceiling for hours instead.

I rub my hands over my face and through my hair taking a deep breath and blowing it out. "How in the actual fuck did I get myself into this mess."

It's got to be approaching dinner time at this point, the sun looks like it's beginning to set. I saunter over to the massive closet and find a comfy crew neck and some joggers to change into. Vince is sadly mistaken if he thought I'd be wearing anything other than comfort clothing while I'm stuck here.

I walk over to the door handle and to my surprise, its unlocked. I pop the door open, half way expecting him to jump out and shove me back inside. I peek my head out and look from left to right but see nothing.

Deciding I've really got nothing to lose, I make my way out into the hall way. It's dark and long with my door being the last one at this end so I head in the only direction that I can.

There are a series of doors, each of which hold a queen sized bed and some other mundane bedroom furniture, nothing personal. Each bedroom is the same as mine, cream fabrics and paint with black features and trim. It's elegant and modern if not a little boring.

The room I'm staying in is the largest by far, I haven't seen the same closet or bathroom in any of the other rooms either. I did find a few bathrooms that mirror mine but with empty drawers and no personal belongings in the showers or cupboards.

I've never understood the point of this size of house with no one to fill it. Other than flaunting your money, of course. Vincenzo said were on an island so I'm not sure who he's showing off for but he's clearly ego driven and maybe a bit narcissistic as well, so I really can't be surprised.

After passing a large circular staircase in the middle of the hall I reach a door on the far side that's locked. It's the only door on this side of the staircase and I presume it must belong to the man himself.

I jiggle the door handle a few more times but its gets me no where. I notice a small black box on the other side of the door. There's no buttons but I poke at it anyways. The box lights up red and beeps quickly three times.

"A fingerprint scanner, on a private island? Really?" I speak aloud to no one but myself.

"Well, it seems necessary now doesn't it?" Noelle, the chef or maid, whatever she is, stands behind me and I nearly jump out of my own skin. I quickly gather myself and straighten my spine.

"Just exploring my fancy prison." I spit out, not bothering to fake a smile. I don't care what Noelle thinks of me, but I do hope she doesn't spit in my food.

"I would hardly call the estate a prison, Ms. Woodruff." I can tell she is annoyed with me now but does she really expect me to be grateful for the nice room? He literally stole me in broad daylight. Even though every time I think about going back home it makes my skin crawl, he still abducted me. He gave me no choice in the matter, just like everyone else around me.

I debate arguing the cold-hard facts with the woman but ultimately decide against it, as she is obviously very loyal to the man who owns the island and everything on it. She's a cute older lady with a high gray bun on top of her head. She's dressed in comfy black pants and a floral button down shirt.

"Just because it sparkles like a diamond, doesn't mean it is." She nods her head not wanting to argue with me either. We both have a point here.

"If you say so Ms. Woodruff. I was just going to prepare dinner if you'd like to join." She turns on her heal and heads for the staircase.

I shrug my shoulders and follow.

Why the hell not?

The kitchen is immaculate. There are three stoves with six burners each. A pizza oven in the far corner and a large island in the middle with chairs on only one side. The counters are all white granite with black trim and fixtures. I've hardly seen an ounce of color in the house beside the emerald green towels and wash cloths in every bathroom.

"Do you eat meat, Ms. Woodruff?" She asks in a tone that is nothing but business.

"Yes, I do. Please, call me Violet." My last name is a constant reminder of the family I wished I had opposed to the one I was given.

"Okay, Ms. Violet. I thought maybe you were a vegetarian since I've thrown away the meals I've delivered to your suite." She thinks I don't like her food. Im starving, actually. I was throwing a fit over my current circumstances but since my captor is gone I suppose it wouldn't hurt to appease my appetite and the nice woman cooking for me.

"I'm sorry, I was throwing a tantrum. It smelled and looked delicious." Why not make friends with the one other person I've seen in the castle.

"I suppose since it is just us tonight, we could have whatever we'd like." She says with a warm smile and a wink.

Noelle and I spend the next several hours making home made dough, rolling it out into crusts and decorating our own pizzas with more toppings than I could have dreamt. I'm not a bad cook by any means, but I'm definitely not a dough from scratch type of girl.

The pizzas take a while to cook. Toward the last ten minutes Noelle goes out to the patio off from the kitchen between the house and water to start a fire in the huge outdoor fireplace.

I take note that she left the door open for me. I guess there isn't really anywhere for me to run anyway but that gesture still strikes me as odd.

She comes back and gives me a warm jacket and some cute earmuffs to match. I throw them on and we take our pizzas out to the table.

We sit in silence and eat while we watch the sun go down over the horizon. I'm comfortable, I enjoy her presence. I don't spend a lot of time with anyone other than Brad and Victoria. So I thought it might be awkward sitting out here with this woman I've just met, but it's not.

I couldn't tell you the last time I had a meal with anyone else. Even when I was home visiting my parents we didn't eat together. My mom hardly eats. I'm not sure if she's got a disorder or if it's the alcoholism, maybe both. My dad can't keep his dick in his pants long enough to be bothered to attend a sit-down meal with his family. He spent most of the week at his office and I'd only hear him sneak in to sleep in his own bed. Now that I think about it, I'm pretty sure out of the entire time I was there I only saw him at Vic's funeral.

Shaking the thoughts from my head I turn to face Noelle, "Can I ask you a question?"

"You can, but I may or may not answer it." I'm not even mad at the answer. I don't know many people who care as much about others the way she does. Considering the fact I just met her and only have today to judge her character, that's saying a lot.

"Where are we?"

"We are on a private island nestled in the middle of lake huron between Michigan and Canada." So that explains the weather and the beautiful autumn scenery. Growing up in Michigan and having spent my entire life there, I am no stranger to the weather.

Speaking of, It's getting colder by the minute now that the sun is gone. Noelle notices me shiver a little.

"Lets go inside, Ms. Violet. I'll run you a bath." Run me a bath? I know she's used to taking care of Vince but I don't need that type of servitude. In fact, I don't want it.

"Its okay Noelle, a bath sounds nice but I've got it." After I speak the words I realize there is no bath in my room. I've been dying to take one since I woke up here yesterday afternoon. "Is there a tub somewhere I could use?"

"Of course, I'll show you the way."

I follow Noelle down a series of hallways, we've taken multiple turns and descended a few more small sets of stairs. I believe we also passed what was the front door. It's got the same box next to it that Vince's bedroom door had.

The fact that I've thought of this place as a house is laughable at this point. It is nothing short of a castle fit for a king.

"Here we are." She stops and opens a large wooden door, gesturing for me to go in ahead of her.

The room is different. The walls are matte black and the jacuzzi tub is black with a satin finish. The floor is a marble black tile with glittering gold grout. There is a floor to ceiling oval mirror surrounded by satin black vinyl trim.

The room is kind of frightening, but beautiful. The towels hanging by the tub are a dark blood red and the varnished golden chandelier looks like it has hundreds of candles attached. They are all glowing a warm orange hue.

The Jacuzzi itself is surrounded by candles of all different heights. Noelle turns the faucet on for me.

"How do you like the water, Ms. Violet?"

"Like I'm in Hell." I'm wondering if I just stepped through a portal and that's exactly where I am. She nods and adjust the water accordingly.

As soon as the door shuts, I lock it. I feel a little guilty for locking her out but I literally have no idea where I'm at in this fortress.

I strip down to nothing and step over the high side of the jacuzzi tub and into the water. I lower myself down slowly. The water is scented with lavender bath salts and and a slightly minty soap. I let some of my signature heinous thoughts swirl through my brain as I lay my head back and close my eyes.

Maybe it wouldn't be so bad to rule in Hell with my own version of Hades.

9

Violet

For three days now my life has been nothing but books, baths, and food. I can't say I'm irritated about it. Noelle and I have been building what I would think could be called a friendship. She doesn't answer most of my questions but I have figured out that Vince and Noelle were born in Italy and that he built this house ten years ago, bringing her with him to work as his chef and head of house. The circumstances in which they met are still a mystery to me but I've come to find that Noelle is a bit mysterious herself.

I like it.

I've actually found that there's a whole staff of people who work here. There are a few houses on the island where they stay. Vince told them to take a few days off when I got here but they came back yesterday. Including some guards and a few housekeepers that came and cleaned my room for me today. I was glad to see Noelle isn't solely responsible for cleaning up after Vince.

Its morning now and I'm in my new routine with Noelle. Were prepping different meats, cheeses, and vegetables for omelettes when I hear a heavy door slam down the hall. At first I don't think much of it as there is people coming and going at all times. However the staff typically use the patio door connected to the kitchen, where we are now.

I stop shredding the cheese in my hand to glance up at Noelle. "What was that?"

"Eh, probably Mr. Bianchi or Matteo." I can tell she's feeling more comfortable with me now because she's been less formal and her accent has been a bit heavier. She doesn't seem the slightest bit phased by the murmuring of curse words coming from down the hall.

"Matteo?" I thought I'd met everyone. I don't remember all their names but I think this Matteo may be someone of importance if he's using the front door and walking through the place like he owns it.

"No one important, Violet." She continues pairing the veggies.

"No one important?" A deep male voice mimics from the door way, throwing his hands to his heart. "You wound me, Noelle." Matteo is handsome, he looks like Vince but, friendlier. His eyes are bit more muted and hazel where Vince's are a striking green. He's covered in tattoos and his hair is long on top but slicked back.

"And who is this fine young lady?" He says walking toward me and leaning his back against the counter next to me so we're facing each other.

"Don't Matteo, unless you want your head on a silver platter, served for supper this evening." Noelle points her small knife in his direction.

He throws up his hands in defense, "No worries, Violet. While you are a beautiful girl, Vincenzo and I have opposite tastes in women. I like mine a bit more…. Manageable." He says with a smirk.

My eyes shoot up to his. "Manageable? You've got to be fucking with me."

"I mean, I don't think you'd be having much more fun at home with Brad, now would you?" He winks at me and walks toward the fridge, grabs a beer, and sits at the island.

The nonchalant use of his name sends a shiver down my spine. I try not to let it show on my face that it shook me.

Cool, another person who knows a lot more about me than I'd like.

"You know what? You're right. But I'd be in a familiar place knowing where I stand with a guy that doesn't pretend not to be a fucking douche bag." I keep my tone light like I'm having a conversation with an old friend.

"Ah, there's the spice Vince was talking about." He smiles harder showing a dimple on his right cheek. He bites his bottom lip and pushes his chair out. "You know violet, you seem like a lot of fun. I should go before I get myself in trouble." And with that he's gone.

"I'm sorry, Violet. Matteo is an *idiota*." She huffs out a breath. "He is Mr. Bianchi's cousin and he lives on the grounds."

"Does he 'work' with Vince?" I put a little emphasis on the word work, I'm not sure if I'd call murdering people for money work.

"Oh no, Matteo is as stealthy as a pregnant Hippo. He is head of security on the island. He does the hiring and manages the staff." We're back to making omelettes for everyone now.

I don't respond. I'm not a fan of Matteo and I don't think Noelle is either.

"Vince does have a small team that accompanies him on his work. Carlos, the pilot for his small private plane, and Lorenzo his younger brother and second in command." Noelle takes my hand. "You will learn to fit in here, I promise." She gives it a gentle squeeze before she lets go and heads over to flip the omelettes she has cooking on the stone griddle.

I don't bother telling her I don't fit in places. I appreciate her guidance and friendship the last few days but I would be naive to think anyone in this house would think twice if Vincenzo murdered me, shoved a brick in my ass, and threw me in the lake never to be seen again.

I head back to my room, the thought of Brad and my inability to form a real bond heavy on my mind. My appetite is ruined now and I just want to lay down. I strip off my athletic-type clothes and throw myself on the bed in my sports bra and underwear.

I can't even think about what Brad will do to me if I return at this point. I could tell him the truth that I was kidnapped and held against my will and he would still find a way to turn it around on me. According to him, it would surely be my fault one way or another.

I changed my clothes after leaving the house that morning and if Vince sent me home in the high waisted leather skirt and blank cropped tank I was wearing, that would be my last day for sure.

The whole reason I've been biding my time in this house and truly trying to enjoy myself is because either way, I'm done for.

This can go one of two ways: 1. Vince gets sick of my shit and finally kills my ass or 2. Vince returns me to my less-than-loving fiancee and he murders my ass. So you can see the dilemma I'm having now. So fuck it, might as well enjoy the cuisine and luxury bathrooms.

I don't mean to fall asleep but the mental gymnastics I do with myself really take it out of me sometimes. I roll to face toward the lake windows, its become my favorite view, but halt when I realize there's a body next to me.

"What the fuck?" I almost scream. I mean I know this is his house and all but Jesus.

Vince throws a hand over his eyes and rubs them both roughly. "*Amore Mio*, I didn't get much sleep on the plane keep it down."

He throws his arm over my side and pulls me close. I try and wiggle away but his hold is relentless.

I close my eyes and pinch the bridge of my nose, "I think you got lost on your way in, Vincenzo. Your room is on the other side of the fucking hall."

I can hear him snicker quietly to himself. "I saw that you tried to use my key pad, if you wanted to get into my bedroom, Vi, all you had to do was ask."

He's smiling now with his eyes still closed and I'm not sure what's wrong with me but I can't stop thinking about how handsome he looks with the golden sunlight shining on his face. His wavy hair is ruffled on top of his head and I want to run my hands through it.

"You wish. Can you let me go? I have to pee."

"So sexy, *Mio Angelo*, say it again." Sarcasm evident in his husky voice. He gives my waist a small squeeze and then lets me go.

I hop out of bed and walk to the bathroom.

"Sway your ass like that in front of me again and we won't leave this bed for a week, Violet. Not even too pee." His tone is stern now and I shut the door quickly.

I press my back up against the door and my heart skips a few beats as I lock it. I've never felt this way about another person, let alone a man that ripped me away from my home.

Although, Brad is the only man I've ever spent time with. He never tried to make me like him. On my sixteenth birthday he came to my house, ate dinner with my family and his, and then took me out to his car. There, in front of my home, he let me know he was owed my virginity and soul he planned to collect in full.

Brad fucked me while I cried in the back of his range rover that night.

I knew life was an unforgiving place before that day, but I lost all intent of trying to make it any better after that. I was almost glad Victoria wasn't around to witness me in the shell of my old self. The same body but hollow.

I keep questioning the warm feelings I have when I think of Vince but it seems a little more clear now after talking to Matteo. How could I stay mad at Vince when all he did was remove me from a situation I couldn't remove myself from?

I thought I was beyond saving. I thought I was alone in a world dominated by horrible men. Hell, maybe I still am. But you can't convince me the murderer I just woke up to is worse than any of the men in my life.

Maybe I can reclaim my life. It's been so long since I even considered what I like or what I'd want to do if I was given the opportunity. For two and half years now the only future I've had was to be a piss-poor excuse for a housewife.

I head to the shower and turn it on as hot as I can get it. I turn on some rain sounds and dim the lights. I might be a captive here but I've definitely learned to utilize my amenities.

If there's one thing to know about me, I'm resourceful.

I step into the shower and try to rinse the little bit of happiness I was feeling off.

I suds up the loofah I found under the sink a few days ago and start with my legs. Happiness is fleeting and my brain has been walled up for years. I allow the feeling to wash down the drain with the used up soap.

I can't protect myself with my guard down.

But I don't think I can protect myself from Vincenzo Bianchi.

10

Vincenzo

The trip to Costa Rica was quick and efficient. It took me less than a day to make friends with the locals and identify the target. A quick bullet to the brain did the trick and the 20 grand I found on his person was donated to a small hospital in the city.

The money from the client was transferred without a hitch to my off shore account where I had it transferred to another, and then Enzo moved it to another as always. We have a system and it works seamlessly every single time. I handle the clients, we work together to find the prey, and then we get paid.

Now, I wait to make contact with my next client and avenge them however they see fit.

Typically, I find more creative ways to rid the earth of the scum I deal with but I was desperate to get back home to my girl.

My trip ran a few days over with some errands in the states. At first there were some issues with the marriage certificate due to Violet's status as a missing person. I expected her parents to keep things quiet but I suppose after so many days they were probably more concerned about keeping things persistent with the Endlow's than her actual safety.

Once I had her removed from the database I was able to head to the court house. Unfortunately, there's not a single judge in Michigan that's not on a first name basis with Theodore Endlow.

Deciding to make things personal, I went with his closest friend in the justice system, Judge Slater. For some odd reason the man was less than receptive to grant my wishes. However, when I held my Glock to his bald head, he was able to figure out how to scribble a few quick signatures. I promised him I wouldn't shoot him if he cooperated, so I put my gun away and slit his throat quickly before fleeing his office.

I always have been a man of my word.

I was hoping to get more than a few hours of sleep with Violet but of course my angel had other plans.

I watch her walk, in one of the thongs I picked out just for her, as quickly as she can over to the bathroom.

My cock has been rock hard since I got here and found her sleeping like that with the door unlocked. I wouldn't go as far as to say she's happy here, but she seems comfortable nonetheless.

I hear the lock twist in the bathroom and I can't help but feel a little twinge of hurt. I hop out out of bed eager to see Violet's naked body in the steamy bathroom. Fuck the fact that I've slept probably 8 hours combined in the last 3 days. The sleep deprivation is nothing compared to the despair my dick has been under constantly since I laid my eyes on her curvy little body.

I take a bobby pin off of her nightstand and stride over to the door. I've picked the lock in three seconds flat and am facing Violet's long golden locks hanging down to her supple ass in no time.

It's takes a second for her to register that I'm in the bathroom with her. She turns quickly trying to cover herself. Her eyes glide down my abs to my boxer-covered erection and she swallows hard.

God and I are no longer acquainted as the Devil has made for a better friend, but I plan to worship at the altar that is Violet Elaine Bianchi for the rest of my life.

After removing what little clothing I had on, I'm trying to watch my pace as I walk toward her but I'm fucking eager to feel her soft skin under the water, to smell her signature vanilla fragrance fresh from the bottle.

She doesn't back away or say a word. She's frozen in place with an arm across her chest and the opposite hand over her bare pussy. In the months I've been watching her I've never seen her shave. Not that I have been able to watch her 24/7 for the last 6 months but I have deduced it to laser hair removal.

I close the distance between us and remove the body wash from the shelf in the wall, squeezing an adequate amount into my hand. I can feel the skin of her stomach brushing lightly against me and my balls tighten.

I suds my self with the sweet smelling soap and then angle the shower head she's using toward myself to rinse off.

"Hey, what the hell?" She gasps. "There's literally three other shower heads and I'm freezing!"

"Don't be a water hog, V. We can share." I catch her wrist as she starts to shuffle to the over head spray coming from the center of the shower.

"I said we'll share this one." I can't let her even a foot away from me right now. The pheromones wafting around her my favorite aphrodisiac.

"Fine." She stands still next to me with both arms crossed over her tits.

"Good girl." I lean my head back and close my eyes as I wash the soap from my hair. "Turn around."

"Do you ever ask nicely? Or am I just expected to do whatever the fuck you say, whenever you say it?"

I stop the smile from forming on my face. "Do you want the answer to that or was it a rhetorical question?

"You're unbearable." She rolls her eyes. I can tell she's trying her best to act perturbed and not stare at my dick.

"See something you like, *Mio Angelo*?" I almost laugh out loud at the way her face reddens and she turns around faster than I expect. "I didn't take you for a prude."

"I'm not a prude, we barely know each other. Well, apparently you know me but I know nothing about you."

"What would you like to know?" She wasn't expecting that from me, but I'm prepared to give her a little bit of myself in return for all of her.

"How did you meet Noelle?" She turns and bats her thick lashes up at me, obviously wet from the shower were currently sharing but I can't help but wish it were my cum they were covered in.

The mention of my elderly chef helps to kill what thoughts I had of that.

"We met at a restaurant in Italy." I turn her body so she's not facing me and load my hand with the expensive shampoo I saw in her shower at home. "She was working there part time as wait staff and going to school full time to become a chef."

"You worked in a restaurant?" She sounds so shocked, if I didn't know any better I might be offended by that.

"Yes, my love, I once bussed tables as a teen to help feed my family." Her arms prickle at my term of endearment. "Believe it or not I wasn't born a hardened criminal."

"You weren't born a serial killer? Weird." She closes her eyes as I work the shampoo into her scalp thoroughly. She lets out a little moan and her eyes spring open.

"It's okay Violet, relax." I pull her head back and keep massaging.

"So, why did you bring her with you to America?" She asks trying to change the subject. I'll allow it, for now.

"She came to me with a business proposition while she was on the run."

"On the run?!" She practically shouts it at me.

I run my palms over her hair as I rinse it, simultaneously trying to soothe her.

"She killed her husband and needed a place to go. Noelle isn't cutout for prison." She turns to face me now and the look on her face is almost comical. "Oh, did she leave that out while you girls were baking cupcakes this week?"

She slaps my shoulder and I laugh.

"So I'm surrounded by a whole posse of murderers?" We both notice she's no longer covering her chest at the same time as we make eye contact once more.

"How does that make you feel, Violet? You spent your week in the company of a woman who knifed her own husband to death." I pause letting my words sink in.

"Now, you're showering with a man who's spilled more blood than most wars from this century combined."

She's breathing heavily now and her chest is heaving with her arms hanging down at her sides. I know my girl, I know that she doesn't think any less of Noelle. She's probably just irritated that she didn't hear it from the horses mouth.

Violet isn't overly emotional like other girls her age. It's one of the reasons I knew she'd fit in just fine to my less than ethical lifestyle. I don't kill for sport like some may think, I kill those who are unworthy of life. Sick fucks who don't deserve to breathe the same air as my angel.

The recurrent movement of her chest is driving me wild now and I'm running my palm up her thick waist and grabbing a handful of tit before I can even think to stop myself. Her skin is smooth and hot.

I don't think my brain can afford to lose any more blood to my dick at the moment or I might actually lose consciousness.

She whimpers again and I can feel the goosebumps rising on her flesh. I lower my head down and close my mouth around the opposite nipple. I suck hard, grazing my teeth over the firm end.

"Vince, please."

"Did you miss me, angel?" She throws her head back as I move to the other nipple and sucks twice as hard. "Tell me, Violet."

"Yes, Vince. I missed you." She whispers.

Lowering myself to my knees, I move my lips down the satin-like skin of her stomach and pepper kisses over her thighs.

"Open your legs, Violet."

She does so with out missing a beat. It looks like my girl can be a good listener when she wants to after all.

I give a firm bite to the inside her thigh and she releases a deep moan. I bite the other thigh before giving her ass a gentle squeeze with both hands.

She runs her hands through my hair and I shove her back up against the wall. She doesn't fight me and moves her leg when I nudge it up and over my shoulder.

Violet

I'm done asking myself what the hell is wrong with me when I let Vince throw my leg over his shoulder. I don't want to think right now, I just want to feel.

I'm overcome with nerves when I think about the fact that I've never received oral.

I shudder against him when I feel his hot breath against my pussy and relax a little. He moves his nose against my clit, teasing me, and presses his finger lightly against my entrance.

"Fuck angel you smell so good, I need to taste you." He growls and I shift my hips forward in anticipation.

This mother fucker laughs at me.

"Be patient, little one." He presses a finger all the way inside and its pure ecstasy the way he curves it up.

He moves his head forward running his tongue in small circles.

"I'm not a patient girl, Vincenzo. You didn't know that about me?" I mock and he lets out a guttural sound in return. The vibration sends shock waves through my sensitive folds.

"Say it again, Vi." He demands while he works two fingers in and out against that magical spot.

I can't answer him I'm too busy trying to ride his face now. I run a hand through his sopping wet hair and pull his head back a bit so his tongue brushes my clit perfectly.

Right before the sensation almost gets the best of me I glance down to look my captor in the eyes before I cover his face in my come.

Vince pulls his fingers out to hold my hips firmly in both hands and the desperation hits rapidly, forcing an involuntary whimper out of me.

"Say my name, Violet."

In the midst of our intense eye contact I notice the perfect dime sized scar in the center of his forehead. I reach out to run a finger over it when Vince slams those two fingers up into my pussy and I scream.

"Fucking say it, Violet!"

"Vincenzo! Please! Please, don't stop."

For a second I consider his oxygenation status while his face is buried so far into me but the way he's sucking my clit has me unable to worry whether either of us make it out of this shower alive.

He flattens his tongue shaking his head side to side against my swollen clit and I explode. The movement so overwhelming that the only leg I have to stand on is threatening to give out on me.

Vince runs his tongue down around my entrance and back up around my clit until the muscles stop pulsating and then lowers us both to the floor of the shower.

"Lay back, Violet."

I'm not usually one to take direction but something about him sucking the soul from my body has me feeling more compliant.

While I lay back with my hands above my head, he throws his leg over me straddling my chest.

I take a second to catch my breath and look up to find Vince staring.

"Push your tits together for me."

I squeeze my chest around his cock and the velvety feeling sends butterflies through me. He pulls back and thrusts up toward my face where I stick my tongue out to meet him.

"Good girl." He growls. I'm being dominated by a man I just met, that I know is not only a hardened criminal but my abductor, and I've never felt more cared for than I do in this moment.

He thrusts faster meeting my tongue each time. He's holding my hands in place above my head, trying to keep me steady while we slip back and forth.

I can feel him starting to twitch and I know he's close.

"Fuck me, Vince." I encourage him and the intense look on his face lets me know it was the right thing to do.

"This is it, *Mio Angelo*. You are sealing your fate with my come on your pretty face."

I suck the head of Vincenzo's dick into my mouth on his next thrust and close my eyes.

He says there's no going back now, but I don't think there ever was.

11

Violet

After our fervent moment in the shower Vince carries me out of the bathroom and into the walk in closet. He places me on the bench and turns to grab a matching set of pajamas off the shelf. The black silk sleep tank and shorts flowing in his hand while he walks back to me.

Vince slides the towel he wrapped me in down over my shoulders slowly. I know he's watching the rhythmic rise and fall of my chest as he chews his bottom lip.

"Arms up." He demands easily. I lift my arms so he can slide the top over them.

Once situated, Vincenzo leans into my ear to whisper in his hoarse voice. "Stand, Violet."

I stand for him.

I'm afraid if I look away I'll break the spell over us. I'm not sure how fast Stockholm Syndrome can set in or if I'm just starving to feel something after years of deprivation but I don't want to burst this bubble of intimacy I've found myself in with him.

I hold on to his broad shoulders and step in to the shorts held out for me. I'm dressed now while Vince stands before me in nothing but his towel laying low on his hips. I have the intense urge to run my hand up his abs and touch his face but I don't.

Taking a step back Vince breaks our eye contact to lift me up again and heads toward the door holding me tight to his chest.

"Where are we going?" I wonder aloud. I'm not sure where we'd be headed in our current attire. Vince doesn't speak as we stride down the long hallway. I glance nervously down the staircase, not wanting anyone to see me in his arms, but no one is present at the end.

We come to an abrupt stop at the door with the finger scanner. I shift uncomfortably knowing he's brought me to his bedroom. Vince pushes a few buttons and leisurely pulls my index finger up to rest on the scanner. There are some quick flashes of green light before Vince speaks.

"You can access all doors with a scanner now. Including the front door." He doesn't spare me a glance before setting me on his bed.

Now I know for certain that Vince felt the shift happen between us just moments ago. Although we're on an island and there isn't a lot of room for me to plot an escape, his trust is something I didn't know I was craving.

I haven't been allowed free roam of anything in my entire life. Even before my life started to fall apart I've always had to fit in the box my father built for us. Here, on this island, I can be the Violet I want to be, unapologetically. I'm not quite sure who she is yet, but I'm on board to find out.

"Thank you." The phrase comes out just above a whisper. It's not often that I thank a man with sincerity, oddly enough in this moment I mean it.

I sit on his bed and ponder what I'll do tomorrow with my

new found freedom. I think I'll check out my window view and watch the sunrise in person first. I almost want to sprint to the front door now just to feel the breeze again. I haven't been out since I ate pizza on the patio the first night he was gone with Noelle.

"It's nothing. I want you to be comfortable in your home Violet."

It's so weird to hear him speak this way. We've only known each for a few days yet it feels like years. I've fallen into a routine here that I never could have dreamt of before. It's like Vince kidnapped me and dropped me off in an alternate reality.

The only fear that this man, this cold blooded killer, brings me is fear of the unknown. Fear that one day soon I'll have to go back to the colorless void I was living in before. The thought alone is enough to break my forehead out in a cold sweat.

It's apparent that Vince can sense my unease when he speaks again. "I brought you in here so we could talk."

"I know you've been looking for answers and I'm prepared to give you some in return for your trust."

I nod but don't say anything. I want to hear what he has to say without prompting.

Vince sits next to me on the bed and glances over at me.

I'm not sure what he's planning to let loose right now but I have a feeling I'm in for a ride.

12

Vincenzo

"How close are you to Theodore Endlow?" I ask wanting to make sure she isn't at all. I'm fairly certain she has no idea what kind of business the man runs on the side but I plan to find out today for sure.

"I'm not." Her short reply leaves room for question.

"Why?"

"What do you mean why? He's my fiancees dad. Why-" I cut her off before I lose my shit.

"That piece of shit isn't your fiancee." She looks shocked that I cut her off, not that I'm declaring her engagement null and void.

For the first time since I took her I see her glance down at her ring finger. I brought her here several days ago and she's just now noticing that the gaudy ring she wore is gone.

"Did you think taking my ring would mean I'm no longer engaged? I'm a human not a stray puppy. You can't just decide because you found me in the street unattended that you're keeping me!"

I consider my answer carefully not wanting the conversation

to stray too far. That's exactly what I plan to do.

She is mine to keep.

"I did you a favor, Violet. Don't take it for granted." I continue not giving her a chance to speak. "Do you know what Theodore does for a living, *Principessa?*" She scrunches her face a little at my question.

"Don't talk to me like I'm 12. I know what he does for a living. You know what he does. People in Mexico know." I wish I could enlighten her to the accuracy of that statement. I just took out Theodore's chief of command for his operation in Mexico last month.

"I'm not talking about his fancy little law firm, love. I'm talking about the after-hours business. The real 'money maker' if you will." I can tell the confusion etched across her face is genuine.

Good.

"I don't understand."

"He is the head of a multi-billion dollar sex trafficking ring shipping girls throughout over 20 different countries I've traced so far." She pales further.

"That can't be true. He's a lawyer, he literally works for the law. Not every single person with money has to be a criminal." I laugh at the irony. It's not her fault she's been sheltered her whole life. It's funny that she thinks the one-percenters actually work hard for their money. Maybe in some aspects they do but not in the squeaky clean way that she thinks.

"*Mio Angelo*, I'm going to tell you a story."

I put my hand on her bare thigh greedy for skin to skin contact.

"I did not always have the things I have today. I was once a poor young kid working in various different restaurants and cafes in Italy. Bussing tables or sweeping floors, anything really to make a few bucks." She nods so I continue.

"My father ran out on my mother just days after my sister was born. It was just me, Enzo my younger brother, and Sofia the baby. My mom worked many jobs just trying to keep a roof over our heads but it was never enough."

Violets eyes are piercing my soul now, she's so enraptured in my story I feel compelled to tell her more than I had originally wanted.

"As we got older I dropped out of school to help support my family and make sure my siblings were able to focus on their studies and make a life for themselves."

"As soon as Sofia was old enough she insisted that she should come help in the kitchen when she had occasional free time." I clear my throat the memory feeling stuck back there.

"One day after closing, Sofia waited so I could walk her home. She was riding her bike ahead of me when a black town car stopped and grabbed her. I ran as fast as I could but the man in the passenger seat stepped out and put a bullet in my head before I could get to her."

She puts a hand to her mouth and glances up to my forehead. I knew when she saw the scar in the shower that it was the right time to get the ball rolling.

"Sofia was only 14 when they took her. The police told my mom they had exhausted all of their resources after only 3 days of searching." I pause for a minute and take a deep breath.

"My mom killed herself the following week. When I finally woke up from a coma 10 days later it was just my brother and I."

Violets eyes sparkle with unshed tears. I know she wants to reach out and comfort me but she is still at war with herself over her situation. I don't look into too deep as I go on.

"In fear of whoever took my sister finding out I lived through his attack, my brother and I changed our names and we went our separate ways. Enzo joined the military. I changed my name to Vincenzo Bianchi, started working for the Cosa Nostra, and never looked back."

"Like the mafia?" A grin tugs on my lips at her wide eyes. Out of all the things I just said she is most shocked of my involvement in the mafia.

"Yes. You don't just wake up one day and decide to become the best homicide enthusiast your time has seen. It's an art really. One I've practiced and crafted for many years." I wink at her and she rolls her eyes back at me.

"What was your name?" Her cheeks blush and her eyes evade mine. She's embarrassed she asked, she knows the consequences of such knowledge.

"Luca." I breathe out. It's been a long time since I said that name. "Luca Rossi."

I hold her gaze for an intense moment until I decide I'm ready to continue on.

"It was Theodore's men who took my sister that day, angel. I knew he wouldn't be anywhere near as effected if I took his wife so I followed Brad while I concocted the right plan to bring his operation to its knees, but then I found you." My look more serious now. The years I've spent tracking this man, pinpointing dealer after dealer to get to him and now it's all right here in the palm of my hand.

"I can't let the Endlow's live. Not Theodore or his son."

She starts to interrupt me but I cut her off. "Don't defend that piece of shit to me, Vi."

"I wasn't going to. I couldn't care less about a single person in the family. But how am I supposed to help you?" The inquisitive look on her face keeps my demons at bay for the time being.

"We will figure that out in time." I say and I mean it. I'm not sure how involved I want her.

"Okay."

"Okay?" I repeat like a damn parrot. Violet's eyes look like they have a hint of a smile but her mouth doesn't reflect the same. I'm sure she's stuck in that beautiful head of hers, fighting only with herself.

I give her thigh a squeeze and stand up, finally shedding my towel and walking to the closet for some sweats and a shirt.

I turn and notice her looking me over with hooded eyes. "Careful. You're making me think you like my company."

She snaps her eyes away from my body and up to mine quickly. "How about you go downstairs and have Matteo walk around with his cock out and we'll see if you look at it or not."

I pause for a second and then finish pulling up my grey sweats. "If I hear another mans name and the word cock in the same sentence come out of your mouth again, I will show you what it's like to choke on your words, Violet."

I watch her throat as she swallows hard. She can't hide her bodies natural reaction to me. Her face and chest is flushed now, contrasting so beautifully with the black sleep set. She stands up but I stop her from moving. "Where do you think you're going?"

"I'm ready for bed." She replies nonchalantly. Even though we just took a decent nap in the spare bedroom, it's getting late and we've exerted ourselves over the past hour.

"You'll sleep here from now on." It's not a question. I can see the argument brewing inside of her racing mind, but she hesitates.

"Okay." She says turning for my side of the bed. I don't mention it, she can sleep on whatever side she wants. I make a mental note to grab the gun out from underneath the pillow, though.

"Good girl, Violet." Her cheeks redden further and she looks away.

I can't say I have a conscious or morals but I do believe in karma. I know by those standards I don't deserve good things in this lifetime. But now that I have the best thing, I'm determined not to let it go.

13

Violet

I wake up to the sun beaming through the stained glass window in Vince's room. I realize quickly that not only did I sleep through the entire night with not so much as a pillow flip but that I'm glued to Vince with drool.

Immediately I try to be discreet and wipe it away but the chest beneath me rumbles with laughter. I look up mortified to find him staring down at me.

"You know it's weird to watch people sleep, right?" I roll my eyes trying to act unaffected.

"Nonsense. Nothing could be weird between us, *Mio Angelo*." He gives me a quick wink and starts to shimmy out from underneath me.

"Where are you going?" I hate myself for asking as soon as I do. I should, at the least, be playing hard to get with my abductor. I think the face-palm emoji was made for me.

Vince smiles before answering. "Don't worry, no where without you."

He makes a few steps forward reaching his closet in no time and grabs a pair of ripped black jeans and an expensive looking black long sleeved tee. I want to look away while he undresses and then dresses again but I can't. I've been attracted to people before, sure, but I've never experienced a pull as magnetic as this one.

"Go put something warm on." He commands.

"It wouldn't kill you to say please." I'm not really bothered by his words but I've come to enjoy riling him up.

"It might." He snaps back.

"You should of told me sooner. If I knew that's all it would take I would have tempted you when I had less clothes on." I try and roll off the side of the bed but he's hovering over me in no time.

"Ouch, *Bellisima*." He's pretending to be hurt but I know he enjoys our banter.

"I'm no angel, Vince." I don't mean for it to come out so sultry but what can I say? He makes me act like this.

A slow smile stretches across his face. "You are." His eyes search mine, the moment more intense than either of us had planned. "A fallen angel is still an angel at its roots." He lowers his head slowly to touch my lips with his. I close my eyes and let the sentiment wash over me.

I don't know when I started to like Vincenzo, but I do.

I meet Vince around the front of the house in the foyer. He's lacing up some black combat style boots while I put on the matching pair he gave me. I went with a black pair of fleece lined leggings and a University of Michigan crew neck I found in my closet. Vince agreed to let me keep my clothes and and bathroom supplies in my room as long as I slept in his, "ours" as he would say.

VIOLET

Vince stands, holding his hand out to me and I take it. He puts my finger up to the scanner, testing it. When we hear the lock click he pulls me through the double doors and into the brisk fall air. I woke up ready to explore the island, but I wasn't expecting a personal tour from the owner.

We walk down the gravel gravel drive way past his Range Rover, toward a pole barn. Vince punches a code into the box by the door and it begins to lift. Inside there's a large boat, if that's what you want to call it, I'm pretty sure it's larger than some houses near campus. There are a few snow mobiles, jet skis, some type of off road vehicle, and various different shelves with tools and other equipment used to maintain the landscape.

Vince pushes me inside toward the small open vehicle. "Arms up." He insists pulling the harness over my shoulders, clicking it in to place for me. He steps around to his side and hops in.

"Ever been in a UTV?" He asks and I shake my head no. He smirks. "Not very Michigan of you." I roll my eyes at the stupid comment and Vince hits the gas hard jerking me back.

"Lose the attitude, Vi." He gives my thigh a squeeze and we're off.

We drive down a winding path in the woods for a few minutes before we come to the first house on the left near the water. It's modest but beautiful. It's a log cabin style type of home with a gorgeous A-frame surrounded by pine trees.

"This is Noelle's house." He points at it.

I nod, not wanting to raise my voice over the loud motor and rushing wind. We pass a few more homes who I now know belong to the guards, Matteo, and Carlos. We pass a helicopter pad shortly after we pass Carlos' house. I'm assuming they're close for obvious reasons.

At the far end of the island now we're approaching another

mansion. "Who lives here?" The house is unreal. It's made up of mostly windows, with an underground garage that were headed straight for. The house is square with sleek, sharp angles. It's futuristic looking, definitely a lot more modern than Vince's castle.

"Enzo, my younger brother." I should have figured that he would live on the island as well, I guess I didn't put two and two together. "Are you up for meeting the rest of the family?"

I notice a small pang of guilt at his words. Vincenzo's entire family consists of Enzo, Noelle, Matteo, and maybe Carlos. I'm not sure how close he is with the aviator that occupies the island but it seems like they spend quite a bit of time together. The feeling leaves me when I realize I could only hope for the small family he has.

"Vin! I was wondering when you'd bring your girl down." Enzo wraps me in one of the tightest hugs I think I've had.

Ever.

Vince notices my uncomfortable smile. "Sorry Vi, Enzo is a bit of a hugger. Probably the most affectionate criminal I've met thus far." Vince laughs and pulls him off of me, wrapping him in a hug himself.

"Sorry Violet." He sticks his hand out for me to shake. "I'm Enzo. Welcome to paradise." He finishes with a wide grin, stretching his arms out around him.

Does this man not know I've been kidnapped? I mean I can't say I'm having a bad time but he's literally comparing my imprisonment to paradise. Sunbeams and rainbows are practically radiating from this man and this is supposed to be the darkest time in my life.

Except, it isn't.

I've never felt more welcome then I do on this island with

my charming warden, his murderous housekeeper, and his borderline psychotic little brother. I can't remember the last time someone hugged me out of endearment rather than obligation or for a photo-op.

I've been afraid many times since I've been here. Afraid to endure, afraid to feel, afraid to let go. Now that I'm doing all of those things, I'm only afraid to be forced back to the shell of a human I was just a week ago.

Maybe I do belong on the island of misfits.

We stay and talk with Enzo for a while. Vince told him about my love for reading and he showed me his extensive in home library, complete with rolling ladders, his own coding system, and the most comfortable chaise lounge I've ever sat in with a view comparable to the one in my room.

The guys talked business while I wandered until eventually it was time to go. Vince told me Noelle was making *Fettuccine al Pomodoro* and *Tiramisu* for lunch. I hadn't had the former but I know from experience that she excels in Italian cuisine. It wasn't until he mentioned the food that my stomach started to growl.

On the ride back we didn't talk. I enjoyed the scenery and the warmth radiating from the large palm resting on my thigh. I never pictured myself enjoying something so mundane, but then again I never pictured myself enjoying much of my life at all.

The wind is cold on my face, I envision my self in a scolding hot bath when we get home.

Home.

Somewhere I haven't wanted to be for years. I couldn't get far enough. Only, I realize now that I'd never actually lived in a home. I'd lived in houses with familiar faces, but never a home.

We park the UTV and I hop out. "Thank you." I tell Vince. I couldn't possibly narrow down all the things I'm thankful for but I mean it.

I think he knows that these kind of conversations don't come naturally to me so he keeps it short. "You're welcome, *Amore Mio.*" I feel my cheeks blush at the affection in his tone. "Come here."

I walk to him without hesitation and don't stop until were so close I can nearly taste the scotch he shared with his brother earlier. I look up at him eager to hear what he might say next. "Yes?"

He doesn't speak, just lowers his face down to meet mine. I close my eyes and tilt my head up to meet his lips. Only his lips never touch mine. I feel his warm breath on my ear instead. "Run, *Piccola Ragazza.*"

I'm not sure what that means but the danger lurking in his eyes tell me I should listen. I leave no room for pause when I untangle myself from him and run up the drive way. There's a small delay in Vince's footsteps before I hear them pounding on the ground behind me.

I pride myself in my gym habits but I am by no means a runner. Vince catches up to me as soon as my hand touches the door handle and he spins me around. My racing heart stutters when he throws me up against the solid oak. "Your terror is intoxicating, Violet." He runs his tongue up the column of my throat and I tremble in his strong arms.

"I'm not afraid of you." I try to keep my voice steady but he bites down hard startling me.

"Are you sure, *Mio Angelo*? I can taste it." The words potent enough to strip me of my usual composure. I pull Vince's face down to me and kiss him hard. I'm done with this cat and mouse game we've been playing. I'm done fighting the pull between us. I run my hand up through his soft waves and moan into his mouth.

Just when our kiss starts to break the bounds of pleasure leading us into ecstasy the door behind me opens. I nearly fall before Vince catches us both.

"I guess you are taken, aren't you little one?" Matteo cheeses down at me.

14

Violet

"Literally fuck off, Matteo." I resist the adolescent urge to roll my eyes for the thousandth time since I've been here.

"What the fuck is that supposed to mean?" Vince asks questioning us both. No doubt thinking back to the time I mentioned Matteo's cock.

"You left us alone for nearly a week, Vin. Look at the girl." He kisses his fingers like a wannabe chef. I start to defend myself but stop when Vince throws a right hook into his cousin's jaw.

I guess that'll work too.

They're rolling around on the ground now when I see Matteo cast an elbow into Vince's stomach causing him to grunt. It must not have phased him too much since he quickly regains the upper hand straddling Matteo's chest and punching him one last time.

"Enough!" Noelle reprimands the boys separating us. "Come eat."

After this Vince stands, offering his hand out to the bleeding man on the floor helping him up. Don't fucking joke about

Violet again." He says letting go of Matteo.

"Who said I was joking?" Matteo winks at Vince and runs toward the kitchen dodging a fist.

Moments later we're all sitting at the island in the kitchen. I wanted to sit in the dining room but Noelle insisted it was too formal. I haven't seen Noelle and Vince interact much before today but I've noticed that there relationship is definitely that of a mother and son.

Noelle brings the hot pan over to the table to scoop some onto everyone's plates. The dish smells and tastes amazing to no surprise at all. I devour my plate in 5 minutes flat ready for the rich espresso dessert.

After we all finish eating I start to help Noelle clean up. "Go on, girl. I've got this."

"You made us a wonderful lunch, Noelle, the least I can do is help you clean up." I insist.

I continue gathering the dishes, setting them down near the sink where Noelle has currently started washing them. Vince sits at the counter watching. "Yes?" I ask, slightly annoyed.

"Just admiring you, *Bella Moglie*." He replies easily.

I start to smile but pause when Noelle drops a glass plate onto the floor behind me. Pieces fly in every direction around us.

"Noelle, are you okay?" I question.

"Vincenzo! Tell me you did not?" Her face is stiff with irritation.

"Don't, Noelle. You know the circumstances of the situation. It was unavoidable." He dismisses her with a wave of his hand.

I'm thoroughly confused by the interaction taking place in front of me. We were enjoying the company of one another and then we weren't. Did Vince say something rude? He's addressed me as such before, I just didn't think to ask for a meaning.

"Can someone clue me in here?" I wonder out loud.

"Certainly, Ms. Violet." She grits out. "Care to do the honors, Vince? Or do you not have such a thing?" With that Noelle throws her towel down and storms out.

"Sit." Vince gestures to the stool next to him.

My feet glide me to him without thought and I sit. I don't speak as I beam up at him in wait.

"*Bella Moglie* means beautiful wife." He says the words with such confidence.

I thought it was maybe a joke but the sincere look on his face has me thinking maybe I'm wrong. "Wife? I don't remember anyone asking me to marry them. Hell, Brad didn't even ask." I joke, saying his name on purpose to rile him.

Vince smiles cheek to cheek, the smile of a psychopath. He stands swiftly leaving only centimeters in between us, but doesn't touch me. My hearts racing now as I think about the severity of the situation. Is it even possible, can you marry someone without their permission? Of course you could. Once a man with reach possesses you, I'm not sure anything is impossible.

"Come, *Principessa*." He tries to rope and arm around my waist but I turn away.

"No, Vince. You aren't going to take me up to your room and pacify me with your pretty words." My head is buzzing. "Tell me what's going on." I demand.

In one fell swoop I'm swept up into his arms and thrown over his shoulder. I swing at his back as he carries me toward the stairs.

"Put me down, Vincenzo! NOW!" I yell, trying to plead with him.

"No." Is the only word he lets out until we reach his room.

Vince sets me on the bed and then starts undressing. Untying his combat boots like nothing happened in the kitchen 1 millisecond ago.

"Care to explain?" I sound like a pissed kitten at best.

"It's simple, really. I can't keep you safe as a Woodruff, so I had your name changed. To mine, of course." He acts as if he barely notices I'm in the room moving on from his shoes to unfasten his belt and find something else to put on. "It was inevitable, anyways. You are mine."

"Yours? Cut the misogyny for just a second, bud. I hardly belong to myself, let alone some stranger granting my family no magical pull or preference in the world." Referring to the pack of assholes waiting for me back in the mitten.

I want to continue but truthfully the only argument that I have, other than basic human rights, is that it was a rude thing to do. Rude to do it behind my back and rude to talk about me like I'm a piece of property.

"Stop!" Vince yells at me for the first time since we've met. "Do not sit here and talk about those people like they give a fuck about you. How about YOU cut the damsel in distress act, huh? Pretending to be locked up in some horrible ivory tower. The dragon isn't always the bad guy, Violet. In fact, he fucking saved you. And he'll turn the world upside down and into ash before he ever gives you back."

I look up at Vince as he stands before me with his chest heaving. I'm pissed that I've never been able to make a single fucking choice for myself. I'm pissed that the choices of others have led me to this exact point in my life.

Mostly I'm pissed that I think I might be falling for the beautiful tattooed dragon of a man in front of me.

15

Vincenzo

I don't mean to yell but I'm done sugarcoating shit for her. Violet is one of the strongest women I know and today I will finally tell her what I know about her fucked up home life. I can see the desire painted across her face but I decide to carry on with what I'm about to say despite knowing it will ruin the mood.

"Do you know why your father gave you away?" The words visibly cutting into her makes me wince internally. "Your marriage to Brad solidified your father's status in the ring, Violet."

"You don't know what you're talking about, Vince." She tries to push me away but I don't budge.

"Why do you think your parents allowed Victoria to leave for years? Do you actually think a man like your father would allow that? They forced her to go, Violet. Just like they forced you." There's no easy way to tell someone that their father sells young girls for a living. She's an intelligent woman, she'd had to have noticed the finances weren't adding up.

She shakes her head. "Fuck you, Vincenzo. Just because my

family is unconventional doesn't give you the right to strip away any good I had left of them." Her eyes well with tears but she doesn't let them fall.

"I wouldn't lie to you, Vi."

She straightens her spine. "You know what, Vince? I'm not doing this. You want to keep me here as your pretend wife then more power to you. But I don't have to sit here and subject myself to this while you take your daddy issues out on me. Maybe call a therapist." She stands up and heads for the door.

I tip my head back and let out a deep laugh, producing a look of horror from Violet. "Sit down, *Mio Angelo,* before I lose my temper." She continues to walk toward the door.

With the press of a button on my nightstand, the dead bolt on the door latches. She tries the handle a few times and then spins to face me. "Fine." She crosses her arms "Keep me in here as long as you want. You won't change my mind."

I'm sure her defiance is not having the effect she desired when I have to reach down and adjust myself in my pants. "My issues happen to be with your daddy, Violet. I don't appreciate men buying and selling young girls. Surely you don't either?"

"You have no proof that my father is involved." She says pointedly, swallowing hard.

"Is your drunk of a mother not evidence enough? Maybe the gated community and mansion? Endless trips around the globe? None of those doing it for you, *Amore Mio?*" I walk over to meet her where she's standing against the door. "Hm, how about the fact that Victoria found out she was next? Leaving without a trace, not to be seen again for two years." I slam my hand on the door next to her head making her body jolt.

"Is it adding up now, Violet? Your twin was of no use to him. She never would have accepted a marriage to another heir of the trade. Her death was only collateral damage." She pales at the mention of her sisters untimely demise. I don't mean to speak of it so callously but she has to understand the severity of the situation.

A lone tear slides down Violet's cheek. "How do you know all of this, Vince? Did you hurt my sister?"

The hurt in her eyes rips right into me. "No." Is all I say, truthfully. But I'm not in the mood to hash out the details of my deal with Brad. All she needs to know right now is that I didn't kill Victoria.

I think back to that pivotal night. When I saw her limp, lifeless body in the frat boys bedroom it was apparent from the bullet hole in her temple that she was gone. Still, I checked her pulse to confirm it before I left her to be found by the next unwilling victim. I didn't think it would be Violet.

I watched from the closet as Violet ran to her sister and sank to her knees. She didn't notice the head wound covered by Victoria's dark hair. Brad quickly pulled Violet up and away from her twin, called 911 and removed her from the room. Judging from the last half of his payment reaching my bank account he thought it was me who took her life.

A few days later I was able to hack in to the departments records and download the autopsy report. There was no mention of a gunshot wound and her death was ruled a suicide. Just like that, all hands were declared clean.

"I don't know exactly what happened, Violet." It's partly true, I don't know who shot her twin. "But I promise to figure it out while I rip this operation apart." I kiss her cheek soaking the saltiness into my lips.

Violet lets her head fall into me and I scoop her into my arms. "You just said they are powerful enough to run an international trafficking ring, how are we going to stop them?" Her big blue eyes searing into me.

I lean in to whisper. "I will rip each Endlow limb from limb until they're extinct." The smile on my face keeps her frozen in place. I don't mention the Woodruff's days are numbered as well, we can argue about that later.

"You might see me as a murderer, Vi, but really I'm just a glorified janitor. Cleaning up the trash littering our planet. Think of it as decreasing my carbon footprint." With that she punches me in the shoulder and rolls her eyes.

There's my girl.

16

Violet

This morning I woke up in Vince's arms again. I've never been much of a cuddler but I can't deny the fact that before I met him I hadn't slept so soundlessly in years. I've learned so much, too much maybe, over the last few days solidifying that I still feel safest here with him.

My parents and the Endlow's are literal monsters. I cant comprehend it. How could I have spent so much time with, ate with, *lived* with these people and not noticed the evil lurking beneath the surface?

I think back to the days my mom was so intoxicated we'd find her sleeping on the tile floor after school or even all of the nannies my sister and I went through. Back then I had thought they couldn't deal with my mother, maybe Victoria's attitude was just too much for a young college student juggling school, work, and a social life. Now, I don't think the situation is so innocent. The thing is, my father and Theodore have endless resources. They know the president for fuck's sake. It's no wonder they are able to keep themselves bright and shiny for the public, whilst disposing of young girls.

I don't jolt out of bed today. I keep my ear to Vince's bare chest and listen to the strong, steady beat of his heart. I trace a finger over the words and symbols on his abdomen. He's covered in dark, decadent ink. I've seen the man naked a handful of times now and I swear every time I do I spot something new.

"Good Morning, *Bella Moglie.*" Running a hand through my hair, Vince breaks me from my trance with his deep voice. It isn't until he runs his hand down my back that I notice I'm topless.

I shrink back to cover my chest but he's to quick.

"Don't you think we're past that?" He cocks and eyebrow in my direction, eliciting a zing of heat to my core.

"I'm pretty sure it's illegal to undress someone without their permission." I roll out of bed, pulling the blanket with me and head toward the bathroom.

"There are no laws on my island, Vi." His gaze is strong and threatening. "Sit."

I'm just inches from the safety of the bathroom but, against my better judgment, I opt to oblige him. I'm sick of being bossed around by him so I decide to try and teach him a lesson instead. I don't think twice before plopping down to my knees on the floor next to the bathroom door.

Fighting a smile Vince adjusts himself in the bed so he's sitting on the edge facing me now. Something snaps in the air around us and the tension rises.

"Drop the sheet." His gaze intensifies and I pause. "Now."

I hesitate for only a second before dropping my hands down to my sides letting the sheet flow out around me.

"*Brava Ragazza.*" My belly twists with nerves. Between the way he's looking at me and his smooth Italian words I can feel my panties dampen. Vince opens his legs a bit more, allowing room for his growing cock. I can see the massive outline dying to burst through the opening in his boxers. He leans back and pats his thigh. "Come, Violet."

Maybe a little too eager to see where this is going, I start to stand but his voice cuts through the thick atmosphere like a knife.

"No." He grits out and then nods once gesturing to the floor. "On your knees." I scrunch my eyebrows in confusion but start to lower myself back down to the plush carpet beneath me.

"Crawl to me, angel." I don't stop to question my sanity or standards before my palms meet the soft ground. Slowly I make my way to him, tits swaying with each move forward. A deep growl leaves his throat as I get closer.

My face meets his legs and I drag my eyes up his powerful body until I meet his. Our intense gaze locked until I skim my hands up his legs meeting his hips. I hook my fingers into the top of his boxers and pull down just a enough to free his dick, playing by my own rules.

The tip glistens and I lick the moisture away. "Fuck, *Principessa*." His accent is thick with lust urging me to give him more. I grab the base and suck the tip into my mouth hard.

Vince grabs a handful of hair and helps me bob up and down. His grip is strong but his movements are gentle, loving. "That's right, Violet. Just like that." With his encouraging words and steady grip I take him deeper into my throat. I move up and down over and over, until tears run down my face. "Good girl, a little more, Vi. I know you can take all of it."

His breathing is rough as hid head falls back exposing his throat. The pressure from his hand getting harder until he rips me up and off of him.

Vince pulls my face up and our lips meet. There is nothing

sweet about our kiss. His tongue is rough and invading before he sucks my bottom lip into his mouth. I slide my hands up to his chest and he spins us around. Vince lets up for just a moment to push me back on to the bed before he lowers himself down on top of me sucking my tongue into his mouth once more.

He notices the moment my nipples pebble against him, moving down my neck and biting me hard. He sucks and licks, grazing his teeth all over my upper body before moving down further to do the same to each breast.

Vince pushes himself up to look at me. "Let's see if you're ready for me?" I only nod. I know I'm ready, my thighs are soaked.

He pulls his boxers down and gives himself a hard stroke before pulling my thong down in one quick movement. There's no warning before he pushes two thick fingers into me. "So fucking wet."

My head leans back and a low moan escapes me. I tilt my hips back and forth riding his fingers before he pulls them out.

"Vince, don't stop." I attest, feeling hollow without him.

"The next time you come will be on my cock, Violet." He pushes his fingers into me again only to pull them out and coat himself in my wetness.

"Vince!" I demand.

I look down to his glistening dick and tense up thinking about the logistics of him inside me.

"You can take it, *Mio Angelo,* you were made for me." He answers, like he can read my thoughts.

He circles the tip around my drenched opening and I push down against him desperate for the pressure. I can feel the stretch as he slowly starts to enter.

"Good girl, let me in." He growls. I can tell it's taking

everything in him to hold back. Inch by inch I feel the euphoric burn and my chest draws in hard. "Almost there, Vi."

"Fuck, Vincenzo!" I cry out when I finally feel the pressure of his pelvis on my clit. His full name provokes him further as he pounds into me. I dig my nails into his back and he pushes in to me deeper, harder keeping his pace consistent.

"Yes, right there." I plead with him not to change a thing.

He curves his large hand around my jaw daring me to look away from him. "Beg me, Violet."

The pleasure from the constant grind of his hips and his long cock pushing me close to the edge. I almost forget what he said until I feel him start to let up.

"Please, Vince, make me come." His hand slides down from my jaw to my throat and squeezes the sides tight.

"This is fucking mine, Violet." His movements are relentless now. "Say it!" He shouts at me.

"It's yours." I practically cry. "I'm yours, Vin." The words slip out from me before I can stop them.

I feel him shudder inside of me just as my climax hits me at full force and we come together with that last sentiment still fresh on my tongue. After a few moments he lowers himself down to one elbow and rolls me over on top of him.

My soul was the last thing I had that truly belonged solely to me, but I just sold it to the devil.

17

Vincenzo

I didn't know how much I needed that connection with her until she gave it to me. I've been with my fair share of women, never more than once, and always a stranger. But, now that I've fucked with feelings I'm not sure what to do with the odd proclivities brewing within me. I've been dying to get inside of her and now I don't know if I'll ever get her out of my system.

Our bare skin has us stuck together with sweat as we catch our breath. We lay here for several moments in silence, soaking in the gravity of the situation, before she shrugs off of me to head for the bathroom.

I let her stand. "Need some help?" I question her with a smug grin.

"Not if we plan to leave this room today." She smiles down at me. She's right about that.

"Who said I did?" I pull her back down on top of me, sliding my hands down her back and over her perfectly round ass.

I don't know that I'm capable of the typical construct of love, that kind of light doesn't live inside of me. But, I do know that

Violet fucking Bianchi has poked a hole through my dark heart and now there's something leaking through.

We spend the rest of the day wrapped in my black satin sheets. Noelle brings all of our meals up and I don't bother clocking in.

There's no doubt that this girl will be my undoing.

After Violet falls asleep on my chest I shimmy my way out from underneath her and head to my office. First things first, I turn on the camera and zoom in to watch the rise and fall of her chest. When I'm satisfied with the resolution I shrink the view to the corner, leaving it visible.

I'm not sure exactly how I'll include the angel in my bed into my plans to kill her ex-boyfriends family and her own. Nor am I sure how she'll feel about it. I saved her the gory details that my sister once babysat Violet and Victoria before her father raped and murdered her.

After a while I was able to trace Sofia back to Michigan and the Woodruff home. From there I followed Nicole to a hole in the wall bar and it wasn't difficult to get her talking about the many "nannies" her and her husband employed. A few drinks and she was practically begging to suck my dick. She couldn't be any less like my wife if she tried.

I believe the woman didn't directly bring harm to my sister or any of the unfortunate victims to set foot in that house, however she is just as guilty for standing idly by. While her husband terrorized young girls under the same roof she drank her self into a stupor, neglecting her children in the process, to keep the perfect peace all these material items bring her.

I can't do anything to save my sister from the misery she went through but I can avenge her in any way of my choosing and I plan to do exactly that. I will give her the kindness of a quick death but only to spare my wife the pain of anything more.

I also promised to help Violet figure out what happened to her twin. My first thought was Brad and while I haven't ruled him out completely I do think it's more unlikely. He transferred the rest of the money to my account that night and while I think he's a fucking idiot I don't think he would have paid me to kill Victoria himself. Bringing me to my second best guess, Theodore.

As soon as I found Victoria I began tracing all her phone calls and messages. I bugged her laptop and put a tracker on her car as well. To my surprise Victoria was in contact with Theodore Endlow for the entire two years she was gone. Not only communicating with him but staying in his home and accompanying him on a handful of vacations. Until one day in June when it came to an abrupt stop.

When Victoria came home.

Two days before her murder she hacked her fathers laptop and sent herself numerous files. Once I downloaded those I realized they had the name's and bank account numbers for multiple buyers across the country. The man was stupid enough to have a complete log of all transactions, who exactly took the girl, and when and where she was taken from.

This led me to believe that somehow Victoria figured out what her father and the man she was spending her time with were doing behind the backs of their loved ones. I'm not sure why or how these girls can be so smart but so unaware of their surroundings. Content with living in blissful ignorance.

Not anymore.

Victoria came out of hiding and while I'm not sure what her initial intent was, it quickly switched over to warn her twin of what type of family she was marrying into. She was going to take Violet with her and go. Unfortunately that was a grave mistake that she would pay for with her life.

I shoot a text to Enzo letting him know I need access to Victoria's original autopsy report, not the one ruling her death an overdose, as soon as possible. After that I shut my computers down eager to get back to the goddess in my room.

On my way back I stop into Vi's old bedroom and check the drawer I know her birth control is in. I open the package to see that she's still taking the water pills I replaced the real ones with. I smile thinking about her being so responsible. She's such a good fucking girl.

Violet and I are about to go through some shit, but it's nothing we can't handle.

18

Violet

The last four days have been rapturous. I've slept better that I ever have in my life. I've spent more time eating divine Italian food that I ever could have imagined. I've bathed in luxury salts and soaps in a bathroom that calls to my soul. Mostly, I've spent time getting to know my husband's body in a way I never could have imagined.

My husband.

I haven't said the words out loud but I let them roll around in my brain from time to time, no longer bothered by the phrase. I'm not sure if it was all the orgasms or if I've completely lost it but I can't imagine my life without Vince in it anymore.

It's hard to believe I've only know the man for a few weeks. In other circumstances it would make sense for us to get married at some point.

There is nothing traditional about the man, there's no point in dwelling on that. I've never wanted a big wedding, my maid of honor is dead, and I'd prefer to skip the daddy daughter dance anyways. Now that I think about it, maybe non-traditional is best. I'll just chalk it up to a contemporary twist and be grateful

NO LOVE LOST

I'm not married to someone who hates me.

I woke up alone this morning and decided to shower and then eat breakfast in the kitchen with Noelle. I walk through the door way and her head shoots up. "I wasn't expecting you this morning." She smiles at me knowingly, "What a pleasant surprise."

"I needed a change of scenery, I suppose." I wink back at her.

"Ham and cheese?" She asks. It's my favorite type of omelette. Vince and Noelle both pick at me because I don't like veggies in it. Speaking of the man, I hear steps approach me from behind.

Hands slither up my back to the base of my skull, tilting it up.

"Good Morning, *Amore Mio.*" Vince's kiss is slow and filled with passion. I can feel my face heat knowing that we aren't alone in the kitchen.

I pull back. "Good morning, Vincenzo." He pulls his bottom lip in between his teeth at that.

He slides into the seat next to me and Noelle doesn't bother asking him what he wants. While he was gone she told me he's eaten egg whites with mushrooms, spinach, and organic Italian sausage every single day since she's began cooking for him. Judging by Vince's muscular body I'm not surprised. He's sweaty now, I'm assuming he just got done in the gym before coming up to meet me here.

"I was surprised you left me all alone up there." I tease him. The man hasn't taken his hands off me for a fraction of a second in all these days. He's washed and brushed my hair, fed me, choked me within an inch of my life. How could I not be in love with him?

The thought sends a cold shiver through my body. Do I love him? I can't. It's got to be lust clouding my judgment.

"I thought you might appreciate the privacy. It was the last moment you'll ever have." He grins and leans into me running his nose up along my neck.

I tilt my head back and let free a quiet moan. The light touch sending more chills allover. He starts to nibble on my neck and I giggle at the sensation.

"Okay love birds, get a room." Noelle narrows her eyes at Vince. "Or better yet leave that poor girl alone."

We all laugh together.

I release a sigh thinking about the irony of her words. This man will never leave me alone and for some fucked up reason unknown to me, I don't want him to.

After breakfast I go down to the dark Jacuzzi tub I became accustomed to loving while Vince was gone. I haven't had the chance to use it again since he's been back.

Lighting every single candle surrounding the exterior of the bath I look at myself in the reflection of the giant antique mirror, something I usually don't do. My skin glows, my hair is thick and flowing down around me, even my eyes look brighter. This must be what it's like to be looked after, to know that someone out there cares about you.

I quickly look away as my eyes start to burn. I stopped hoping someone would love me long ago. Even though this man rid me of the terrible life I was living at home does not mean he loves me.

I undress and let my body slide down into the hot water. I close my eyes and push all the thoughts away. I don't want to think or feel right now. I just want to relax and enjoy this small moment of reprieve.

I'm not sure how long I'm asleep in the tub, but when I wake up the water is frigid and some of the candles have burned out. I rub my eyes a few times and pull the lever for the drain.

I grab the gigantic plush towel and let it engulf me. It can't be that long or surely Vince would have came looking.

Leisurely I make my way through the winding halls and up the stairs to the walk-in closet in my old room. Not until I sit down on the bench does it strike me as odd that I didn't pass anyone on my way up. I mean it's usually only Noelle, Vince, a couple guards, and I. But where did everyone go?

Once I'm dressed I step out of the closet to see the sun setting behind the tree's in the distance. It would make sense that Noelle is busy preparing dinner, I guess.

I'm not sure why I feel the need to run right back to Vince, but I do. After I'm dressed I let my feet guide me to his office before I check his room, not wanting to get sucked back into that black hole. I'm freaking hungry.

His office is equipped with the same finger scanner. I lift my index finger to it and the lights flashes green indicating approval. I push the door open but the room is empty. It takes me a few seconds to take in what I'm looking at.

There are screens everywhere. There are business meetings go on, men talking in a small corner at the bar, people arguing and fighting. Some screens only have data and numbers pouring across them. Suddenly something strikes me as familiar. I see a perfect view of my front porch and then I see my bedroom with perfect clarity.

My old bedroom at my parent's house. I haven't lived with my parents since the day I turned 18 and was forced to move in with Brad.

I walk over to the screens and sit down in the high-back leather chair intent on figuring out what the fuck is going on.

Vince's email is pulled up and sitting right there on the top, is a message titled 'Victoria'. My heart hammers against my chest when I hover over it. I hesitate for a second, wondering if I really want to see what's hidden inside.

Of course I do.

I click it open and my eyes widen in horror. Attached are complete, detailed pictures of my sister cut open and splayed out on an examining table. Her skin pale and gray. Her eyes are sunken and closed. Her beautifully colored, brown chestnut hair falling over the edge.

I gasp and throw my hand over my mouth realizing this is from her autopsy. There are more documents attached so I scroll further. The head of the page makes my stomach drop. Cause of death: Gunshot wound to the head.

As I scroll down I see that not only was my sister shot, she was pregnant at the time of her death. My head spins as I try to make sense of the content before me. Vince had to have been looking into my sister's death like I asked him to. He promised to help me find her murderer and he is. I fully believe that until one last shocking thing comes into view.

The same purple case that once covered my sister's phone sits next to a stack of papers on the far side of the desk. It can't be. I flip it over and tap the screen hard, jumping up when it flashes a picture

Twins.

One blonde, one brunette. At their 9th grade homecoming dance with their arms wrapped around one another, smiling with shining white teeth. My favorite picture of us.

Two young, naive girls with no idea what was to come.

I slide the phone into my pocket and I run.

I run with no destination, determined to get out of this

house. I trip and almost stumble down the curved staircase but correct myself just in time. I think I might hear Noelle mutter something off in the distance but I don't stop. No matter what the circumstances are, she will always take his side. I'm alone on this island.

I quickly press my finger to the scanner and bust through the door as soon as the light flashes. I don't bother with a jacket or even shoes.

Immediately the wind whips across my face and I wrap my arms around my body as I jog down the driveway. The leggings and quarter zip sweatshirt I have on do absolutely nothing to shield me from the late autumn weather.

I run and run until my lungs burn and my heart feels like it will give out. I've passed Noelle's house and a few others I think belong to some guards. When I reach a familiar mansion, I rapidly go over my options in my head. Really there's two: dive into the glacial lake and swim two hundred miles or so to shore or ask Enzo for help, I go with the ladder.

I walk right up to his front door and bang ferociously. Only a few seconds pass before I hear footsteps and the door swings open.

"Take me home."

19

Vincenzo

"Fuck!" I yell as I watch Violet flee my office. I had to leave the island for a target in the Upper Peninsula of Michigan. Knowing the trip would only take a few hours, I told Noelle to tell Violet when she was done. Under no circumstances was anyone to disturb her bath.

Enzo let me know that our latest hit had just landed in Michigan earlier in the week, hiding out with family. He's lucky I'm a courteous murderer and waited for his sister and nephew to leave the house before I mutilated him. I cut his tongue out and seared each individual finger print off before dumping him in a river near the house. I didn't think he'd be able to swim after hemorrhaging with cinder blocks tied to his bound limbs, but I stuck around for a bit just to see.

I slam my bloody fist on the chair. "Faster, Carlos!"

I'm such a fucking idiot for leaving that shit up. I always sign out and lock my computers down when I'm done using them. Violet's presence is so distracting, I knew I was bound to fuck this up at some point.

I can only imagine what she's thinking about the autopsy

report and her sister's phone on my desk. The day I found Victoria, I took her phone for collateral. I wanted to know first hand exactly what and who she was talking to. I wanted to go through it with a fine tooth comb to see what I was up against.

I guess waiting for the right time to talk to her about it was a mistake.

"I'm going as fast as I can boss."

I know that but I'm going to vibrate out of my fucking skin if we don't get on the ground soon. I know she can't get far but the thought of her having even the slightest chance of leaving sends a violent rage through my chest.

I saw her leave through the front door and then sprint past the cameras on the pole barn but that's it. There are no more cameras aside from the landing pad and runway.

It seems like and eternity before I her my pilot through the headset. "Going down." Carlos is brief, letting me know so I can brace myself for landing.

As soon as our wheels touch the ground I'm up and out the door. Initially I want to go grab the UTV but it's loud. I don't want to scare my prey. It's dark now and no one knows these grounds better than I do.

I know that Violet won't be in any of the staff houses, they aren't dumb enough to try and keep her from me. There are hundreds of trees on this island but the ground is mostly flat with no caves or alcoves for her to seek shelter in. Leaving only one place to hide with one person stupid enough to try it.

I take my range rover from the runway and park it in the circle drive in front of Enzo's house before I walk down the path to the garage. I punch in the code and watch the door rise.

Striding over to the door leading into the basement I bust

through without knocking.

"Where the fuck is she?" I yell, skipping steps up to the main floor. At first I don't think I'll receive a response, until I do.

"Where's who?" Enzo smiles back at me. I uppercut my brother as soon as he's in reach.

"Don't fuck with me, Enzo. Where's my wife?" Blood drips from the corner of his mouth and he wipes it away.

"Oh you told her she's married? I guess chivalry isn't dead." I swing on him again but he dodges my left hook. "If you can find her, you can have her." He winks along with his nonchalant statement. If he wasn't my little brother and last remaining blood relative I would kill him right now.

"VIOLET!" I shout. "Get the fuck out here!" I try to walk past him but he blocks the door frame. "Lorenzo, I swear to Satan himself." Letting his dead name flow freely with the pent up anger inside me. We never use our birth names, not even in private to reduce the chance of letting them slip in public.

I get in my brother's face but halt when I hear what I think may be my little angel. The footsteps sound as if they're going down stairs, quick but light. I cease all movement, cocking an eyebrow at my brother. His facade falters when he glances behind me to the picture window in his kitchen. Bingo.

I turn, narrowly avoiding Enzo's grasp and fly back down the staircase to the garage. I crash through the heavy door into the brisk fall night weather. Momentarily, I pause to listen for the sound of her steps. I hear something faint over to my right and I'm moving before I can register it, pure primal instinct taking over.

You can run but you can't hide from the devil, little one.

20

Violet

I bartered with Enzo to take me home. I begged and pleaded, I cried and screamed but the man is immovable. I even tried to guilt trip him with the death of my twin, that would work with anyone else, but I forgot the guy's a lunatic.

He told me all he could do was give me some sanctuary from Vince. So I accepted it. I can bide my time and find a way off this island. I saw a boat at the end of his dock, I've never driven one but it can't be that hard. I just need to locate the keys and then I can make a run for it.

I've barley been at his house an hour, finally getting situated in a guest room, when Vince come's bursting through the basement door. I can hear his deep voice thundering through the house. The brother's exchange words before I hear the sound of flesh hitting flesh.

I shiver, feeling guilty for whoever was just injured, before cracking the door to hear what they're saying.

"VIOLET!" Fuck. I panic a little, he's going to find me if I stay in this room. He'll tear this house inside out to get to me. There is no rhyme or reason to his madness and there's no way I can conceal myself from a man who finds people for a living.

I throw on a pair of men's socks I found in the dresser and creep out. My movements are rapid but silent. I sneak past the kitchen doorway and Enzo doesn't so much as blink. I'm certain he could see me in his periphery but his his intense gaze never leaves the man in front of him. I let out a small breath of relief as I inch the basement door ajar and slip through the small opening. Once on the other side of the frame I can't help but dash down the stairs at full speed.

I don't think twice about the men upstairs when I dash out into the pitch black forest. I feel a small twinge in my heart and I have to remind myself that this man may have killed my sister. I let him manipulate me into feeling things for him and I've got to put a stop to it now. I've got to break this bond before it breaks me.

So, I run.

I take off into the woods, opposite the way I came. We didn't venture this way on the UTV but it looks to be purely tree's with no housing or lights. I feel a flutter of fear in my chest but I run without pause. I don't have time to be afraid of the dark right now, I'm running from a serial killer.

After fifteen minutes or so I'm completely out of breath and stop near a large tree wide enough to hide my frame. I sit down and rest my elbows on my bent legs trying to slow my thundering heart. I lean my head back and stare up at the stars. I wonder if my life was always going to end up this way? If I make it off this island will I spend the rest of my days in hiding?

I wave the thoughts away to try and figure out my next move. I can stay here until the sun comes up and make my way back to the dock or I can move from place to place hoping to stay ahead of Vince. Both ideas coming with their own set of pro's and con's. I close my eyes for just a second before I hear a soul shattering sound.

Vince's laugh.

A low, mesmerizing yet terrifying sound that I'm not sure I'll ever be able to live without.

I squeeze my eyes shut tight, silently pulling myself into a small ball against the tree. I try and slow my harsh breaths but his words catch me off guard.

"Don't give up now, Vi. You've came so far." I hear the smirk in his voice, indicating that I really haven't gotten far at all. I should have known I couldn't hide from him on his own island.

I pull both hands up and over my mouth as I hear the footsteps nearing closer. The leaves crunching right behind me now.

"Run, *Bella Ragazza*." A violent shudder racks through my body. His voice a deep whisper near my head now. "Because when I catch you, I'm going to show you exactly what it's like to be my prey."

I don't debate my options before my fight or flight response kicks in. I'm up and on my feet, running like my life depends on it. I'm pretty certain it does. Vince doesn't need my help to get to any of the people I'm connected to. He's got resources and relationships of his own.

My heart races and my lungs ignite with fire but I don't stop. My feet pound against the pine needles and rocks, the socks I stole doing little to protect me. I have to get away from him, I have to find a spot to save my self but I'm too late.

Abruptly, I'm jerked back by my sweatshirt and down to the forest floor. I come to a crashing halt at a familiar pair of black military grade boots. Slowly, I rake my eyes up his legs to the bare tattooed chest I once found comfort on. I blink my eyes when I reach his face. The lower half is covered by a skull mask that wraps around to the back of his head. His beautiful green eyes glow in the moonlight. I'm not looking at Vince, the man who stole me away from my tragic home life.

Right now I'm face to face with Vincenzo Bianchi, the man you call when you need someone wiped from the face of the earth.

I turn my body away, dragging my ass across the ground in a weak attempt to crawl backward. He takes a long step forward, slowly raising his boot up to my chest pushing my back to the ground. "Caught you, *Mio Angelo.*"

The air leaves my lungs as he presses down firmly. I yell as loud as I can, hoping there is someone on this island with a conscious. I try and roll away but it's useless, he presses me down into the dirt until I'm sure my ribs will crack.

"Scream. If it makes you feel better to pretend this isn't what you want, be my guest." I open my mouth to argue with him but stop when Vince takes his boot off my chest, kneels down next to me, grabs my lower jaw and whispers in my ear.

"There's no one here to help you, Violet. It's only me and you, for better or worse." His hoarse voice doing things to my brain that I can't explain. I can tell by the squint of his eyes that he's smiling.

Sick bastard.

I should be fighting for my life right now, doing any and everything to get away from this man. Somewhere deep down I know he didn't hurt Victoria but I don't know who did and I'm not sure I can trust him.

I don't want to think about that right now, I can't. My body won't let me. The steady thrum in my bones too loud for me to think over. The heat low in my belly blinding me from the formidable danger.

NO LOVE LOST

I guess I'm a sick bastard, too.

21

Vincenzo

The burning desire coursing through me is making me not want to let go of Violet's face. I have to remind myself not to crush her delicate bones into dust. I inhale her scent sharply and then turn her to face me.

"I don't make empty threats, Vi." I tell her as I lick the tear running down her porcelain cheek. The salt water does something insane to my already writhing innards. She starts to talk but I swiftly flip her over onto her stomach, straddling her. I have no use for her lies, arguments, or excuses. Today my wife will see what it's like to play games with her husband. It's not something that will stick with her just for today, I have a way of making things attach to the temporal lobe for permanent residence.

I pull her leggings down and off not sparing a second thought to the temperature. The heat flowing through me is enough for the both of us. I use the stretchy pants to bind her wrists behind her back. Using my right hand to unbuckle my belt and twist it once around my hand, in one swift movement I give it a rough pull and it glides through every loop without pause.

I crack it down once on her ass, instantly leaving a red stripe. Violet moans loud and the sound vibrates through her and straight to my groin. I wrap the belt around her neck, lacing it through the buckle. I pull it taught and lean my bare chest down over her.

"Are you ready for me, *Principessa?*" Violet tries to squirm away but between my relentless grip on the belt around her throat and my heavy body on top of her it's a waste of energy.

"Fuck you, Vince. " She grits out in a breathy tone, her face flushed. I can't help but let out a little laugh.

"Oh, I plan to, wife. Today, tomorrow, 40 years from now. You've managed to steal every accessible thought in my brain. Let's do a little experiment. Let's see if I can fuck you out of my system?" I smile maniacally and let out a little chuckle.

I pull the belt tight and push her face to the forest floor. Without warning I run a finger between her ass cheeks and into her saturated hole. "I thought you didn't want me to touch you? Your body is telling me other wise."

I push my finger in and out a few times before adding another. "I didn't touch your fucking sister, Violet. Brad paid me to kill her but I didn't. I promised to help you solve her murder but now I don't know if I'm feeling so generous." She lets out a whine and I'm not sure if it's from my thick fingers stroking that sweet spot inside or because I've considered backing out of our previous deal.

Deep down she knows I didn't hurt her sister. I may not be a good man but I would have to have a damn good reason to kill an 18 year old pregnant woman. Even though she hasn't known me as long as I've known her, I know that she at least knows that.

I use my opposite hand to pull out my rock hard cock. I rub

the head against her back. entrance. "How about this, Violet? Would you run from me again if I fucked your ass right now?" She doesn't answer, only shivering in return. I make a mental note of her reaction but move on.

"You want my cock, *Bella Ragazza?*" I ask her and her hips shift up to rub my aching dick.

"Yes." I can tell she's hating herself for her reaction to me. Her teeth are clenched and her body is wound tight.

I won't allow it.

I lean down to the side she's facing. "You were made for me, Violet. You will feel nothing but ecstasy when you're with me. Do you understand?" I go back to finger fucking her. She doesn't answer.

"Violet!" I yell trying to pull her back into the moment. "We will figure out what happened to your sister. I'll take care of the entire fucking Endlow family and then you and I will live in bliss. Do you understand me?" I'm shouting at her but I don't care. I feel like a fucking crack head. The scent of her arousal does things to me that even a fresh kill couldn't.

"Okay! Fuck." She's panting and riding my fingers. "I understand, Vincenzo."

"That's my girl." I pull my fingers out and replace them with the head of my cock. Violet screams out while I push in all the way in one go. "Good girl, Violet. Look at you taking my whole fucking cock."

I give her a few slow, hard thrusts to let her get use to my size until I can feel her muscles relax a bit. I'm not capable of going easy on her right now, the hunt has me ready to crawl out of my skin if I don't release the pent up energy. I stretch to my full height and pull the belt tight only giving her enough air to keep her alive.

"That's it, *Bella Moglie*." I praise while pounding into her without reserve. I keep one hand on the belt and use the other to scoop up some of her wetness. I take the damp fingers and trail them to her back hole, working the muscle open. She moans at the foreign sensation and then relaxes.

I pump my fingers and cock into her simultaneously until I can feel her pussy start to tighten around me. The pebbles digging into my knees do nothing to alter my rhythm.

"Fuck, Vin. Please, yes, yes!" Violet's orgasm overtakes her violently. I feel her contracting around me and there's nothing I can do to stop myself from following right behind her.

I move inside of her lazily until I know every single drop of cum is pushed deep inside of her. "I wish you could see my view, Vi. You're so fucking beautiful." Once I'm finished I pull out and use my fingers to push any leaking remnants back in. I release my belt from her throat and the binds from her wrists, throwing them to the ground. I move off of her and adjust myself into my pants. I lay down and pull Violet's trembling body into me. We stare up at the stars without speaking for a few minutes, I allow just enough time for us to regulate our breathing

Standing, I scoop Violet into my arms and make my way back to Vince's house where my SUV is still parked. She pulls my face down by mask, tucking it under my chin, and places a soft kiss on my lips. Her eyes close as she rests her head against my chest. Eventually her breaths become more shallow letting me know she's dozed off.

I want to wake her up and yell at her some more, maybe fuck her again. I won't though because my girl is going to need some rest. In a few days when I've fucked the remaining rage out of my system I'm going to take Violet on a field trip back to her

VINCENZO

hometown.

My sweet little Persephone will get to see her husband at work.

"Four fucking hours. I was gone four fucking hours and you run off on me." My chest draws in deep as I try and fail to calm myself. "Should I insert a tracker into your arm and watch your every move like a dog?" It's an ironic statement since I saw most of her tantrum go down on camera, but she doesn't need to know that.

Violet sits up, covering her chest in my sheets. When we got home last night I stripped her bare and laid her in my bed. I couldn't, in the newly found good conscious I've accumulated, sink myself inside her again but I needed to feel her skin against mine nonetheless.

"You're actually mad at me? We're on an island?! Where exactly would I go, Vince?" I don't tell her that she's probably right. But, on the off chance she steals a boat or figures out how to drive a helicopter, I won't risk it.

"It's the principle." I huff out, trying to contain myself. "What about the wild life? Did you have a gun? Mace?" Her face pales a bit, I can tell she didn't take any of that into consideration.

"What if my men wouldn't have recognized you, *Mio Angelo*? Would you be able to stomach the disembowelment of any man who dares to touch you?" I can feel my eyes darken from the fear radiating from her. "I would make you watch as I sliced him open hip to hip and his intestines fell out onto the floor. Could you live with that?"

"Jesus, stop." She closes her eyes tight.

"Then the next time you have a fucking question, you ask. Got it?" My voice is still firm but the sight of her naked, disheveled body tucked into my bed almost has me forgetting what landed us here in the first place.

"Tell me what happened, Vince. I won't ask again if you tell me the entire truth. Don't spare the details, be honest with me. Please." Her eyes are pleading. Despite my better judgment, I give her exactly what she's asking for.

"Brad hired me to kill your sister." She watches my every move as I let the towel around my waist fall, drying myself off from the shower I took while she was asleep. "I started following her in April, as I do with all targets, I watched her for a few months until I could plot my next move. Except this time, I found you. I had to craft my course of action carefully in order to get in with the Endlow's and keep you." I take a deep breath considering how I'll word this next part.

"How much do you want to know about your sister's time away?" I ask her innocently but her brows furrow in anger. I throw my hands up in a mock surrender.

"Okay, okay. She was… seeing Theodore Endlow. Staying at his house, accompanying him out of the country, using some of his credit cards." She stops me.

"What? That's not possible. Victoria hated that family." Violet shakes her gorgeous head in disbelief, her hair swaying back and forth with the movement.

"She was pregnant, Violet." She halts completely, even her breathing discontinues. "Someone shot her in the head at that party. I don't know who or if they knew she was pregnant but we will find out." I promise to her with our eye contact unwavering.

"As for my involvement, I was at that party to see how her and Brad interacted. I needed to know what he knew about her relationship with his father. I needed to know what Victoria knew about the missing girls." Violet gasps.

"You don't think she was involved in that, do you?"

"No, *Amore Mio.*" I answer sincerely. "I think your sister is just as much of a victim as they are. Just under different circumstances. However, that's why I took her phone. I saw her downloading things on to it from your father's office and I needed to see whose side she was on."

She doesn't respond. I can see the wheels turning in her head as she pieces the puzzle together. I'm not going to explain myself further, she knows what I know and that's enough for now.

I give her a few moments to collect herself but when she lets her body glide back down to the bed and the sheet slips exposing her naked tits, her nipples pebbled from the brisk air, that's all it takes.

I can't stop myself before I'm straddling her waist and thumbing her jaw. I lick up the delicate column of her throat and into her open mouth.

"No more talking, wife." And she doesn't. We don't talk again for hours.

After spending a few days in bed and then a few more playing our own fucked up version of hide and seek I decide we've had enough fun for now. We'll only be gone a day or two.

We'll get back to this.

"Go get dressed and wear something warm. Were going for a ride in the chopper."

"The helicopter?" She asks. "Where are we going?" My sweet, inquisitive girl.

"We're going to see what's been going on in St. Lane since you've been gone." I smile at her with wild eyes.

This is going to be fun.

22

Violet

Pregnant. How could Victoria be pregnant by my fiancee's dad? Ex-fiancee I suppose but that's irrelevant. Vic was smart and independent. She never would have allowed someone like him to touch her, let alone knock her up. Did she really change that much over the two years she was gone? Or did I never really know her at all?

I think about the few months we had together as I guide myself to my walk in closet on the opposite end of the hall. I'm not exactly sure what Vince has in mind for us today but I'm almost certain I'm not going to enjoy any of it.

Victoria seemed a little different, of course, but we're adults now. I'm sure I seemed more than a little different to her as well. When she left I was by no means shy but I definitely wasn't as outspoken as her. When she returned, my indifference toward my situation was beginning to fuse it's way into anger. I was speaking my mind more, allowing sarcasm and defiance to leak it's way in staining my once pure demeanor.

The last day I saw Victoria she told me she wanted to speak to me. Who knows if it was regarding the pregnancy or the relationship or something else entirely. It's painful to think I'll never hear the truth from her. I brush the thoughts off with the conclusion that I will get revenge for my twin.

Walking into the closet I grab a comfy pair of jeggings, a white tank with a flannel button down to put on top, and a black puffy vest. The room feels smaller than usual as I lay back on the bench and stare at the ceiling decorated in a beautiful mural complete with clouds and something similar to the island sunset on a warm summer day.

"Ready, Vi?" His dark voice lays over me, cocooning me like my favorite blanket.

I'm not ready, I don't want to go back. That's a feeble thought that I won't let slip.

Vincenzo Bianchi's wife is anything but weak.

"Good morning, Mrs. Bianchi. Welcome aboard." A man, who I'm assuming is Carlos, greets me in a flat tone. His face doesn't change as he greets Vince and Enzo behind me.

"Violet, this is Carlos my pilot and closest friend. Carlos, my wife." He gestures toward me and I shake Carlos' outstretched hand. "We met during my time in the Cosa Nostra." Vin explains as we start to move back.

"Hi." Is all I can manage to say, my intense fear of flying creeping in ready to burn me alive.

"It's okay love, here." I take the water bottle from my husband. He steps around me, letting me lead us to the back of the helicopter to sit. I take a healthy drink of the water hoping the action will some how calm my nerves.

"How'd you know-" I trail off. "Never mind." The man literally knows everything about me, of course he knows I hate flying. I finish the water off and he takes it, tossing it up to

Enzo who smirks and disposes of the empty bottle.

I start to smile back and then I feel it. "Vincenzo!" I yell slapping at his shoulder but the movement is weak, similar to the sensation of trying to hit someone in a dream. "Did you drug me?" I shout over the now rotating blades.

I can't hear exactly what he says, but it sounds a lot like you're welcome.

My head spins for just a moment longer until my heavy lids close on me and everything goes dark.

"Ah, there's my girl." Vince smiles down at me as I blink my eyes open.

"You're an asshole." I try to sit up but my limbs are still incapacitated. My head is resting on his thick thigh and he's stroking my hair back away from my face. I'm glad for the apparent last shred of dignity I still have because I don't purr like a fucking kitten right now even though I want to.

"Slow down, Vi. We're going to eat dinner and talk about our plans for tomorrow. We're in no rush." Between the rhythmic glide of his hand through my hair and his rich voice I want to close my eyes and drift back off into a deep, deep slumber. Since I've been with Vince I've been catching up on years of lost REM cycled sleep.

"Where are we?" The only coherent thought I can form.

"My cabin in the Amber Forest." He replies.

"In St. Lane's?" I ask confused. Why would he have a cabin so close to my house? Until it hits me. "You literally bought a cabin to stalk my sister and I better?"

"Of course not." Vince's chuckle is like the sound of rubbing velvet on velvet, smooth and melodic. "I bought this cabin to stalk *you* better, *Mio Angelo*."

I look away as I feel the blush creep over my chest and up my neck. It's more than confusing trying to work out my feelings for the man. How is it that the person who stalked and kidnapped me is the only person, aside from my twin, that I've ever felt real authentic love for? Not out of obligation or necessity, just pure unadulterated love.

Yeah, I'm fucked. Mentally, physically, emotionally, all of it. Because I love Vincenzo.

It's a sobering thought and I can't hide the visceral reaction that sits me up. As I lift my head up off of Vince's lap, I try and scoot away to gain some mental and physical clarity but he doesn't allow it.

"What's wrong?" He questions.

"Nothing." I grit out, letting my head fall to the side. I really am shit at hiding my emotions when it comes to this man.

I used to have an impenetrable wall built around me, protecting me from the things out of my control. Leave it to Vince to break it down. I'm feeling like a frayed nerve, more than a little exposed.

23

Vincenzo

I watch the dot move on my phone as Violet makes her way down the street to Brad's front door. As soon as the words about installing a tracker in her left my mouth I couldn't think about anything else. While Violet slept in my lap on the helicopter I gave her a quick little injection into her upper arm sealing her fate.

Hardly left a mark.

Now, I'm stationed with Enzo down the road listening and watching from the camera Violet's wearing in her flowy white top on a laptop settled in between us. Her beautiful blonde hair is pulled back in a loose braid that reaches down her spine to the top of her ass. Her shirt shows just a little bit of cleavage while the dark denim jeans she chose hug the curves of her thick thighs and ass perfectly.

It was a struggle to let her out of the SUV but I couldn't exactly go in with her.

I sit back in my seat not taking my eyes off the screen for a second. I can be there in under 60 seconds if she needs me but I'm still on edge. I'm not sure exactly how far I'm willing to let this go but I want her to get what she needs out of it.

Violet steps up to the door to knock and I can hear her breath hitch. She's nervous. I wish I could reach out to her, grab her hand and comfort her. She's stronger than she knows but even the best of us need a little reassurance. By the time I'm done with her she'll realize that while most of our relationship may be a dictatorship, I will always allow her to spread her wings.

Before I know it she's reaching out to the giant wooden door and banging her fist against it, as if she's a stranger and not someone who lived there just a few weeks ago. I can feel my heart pound against my chest as I wait for the door to swing open.

It does.

Brad stands there in nothing but basket ball shorts looking disheveled.

"Violet?! I thought you were dead!" He scoops her up into him, squeezing her against his chest.

"Why?" She asks accusingly. She's got to be careful with her words or he's going to sense that something is off. He's a stupid guy but even he would be able to pick up on the vibes.

"You've been gone nearly a month!" He sets her down gently and pulls her inside. I see just a hint of something I don't like, the wheels are turning in his thick skull. I can only imagine what he thought his own father might have done to her, where he may have shipped her off to.

"Actually, where the fuck were you?" He looks her up and down. "Doesn't look like it's been anywhere too terrible, huh?"

I roll my shoulders in discomfort. I should be there with her. I wish I could see Violet. I squeeze the arm rest hard trying to redirect some energy.

Just as we discussed Violet follows script. "I'm sorry Brad. I needed some time away. Vic's death, school, wedding stuff.." She sighs. "It was too much."

Brad laughs with anything but humor. His chest is rising and falling rapidly. "You didn't answer me, Violet. I said where the fuck were you? I won't ask again."

"I was with my aunt Alison in Colorado. You know, the one in the mountains?" Careful, Vi. Too much detail is a sign of deceit.

"Hm, so aunt Alison, who you haven't spoken to in years, aided and abetted a runaway?" He mockingly lifts a finger to his chin. I can feel rage settling low in my abdomen, my demons begging to be called to action. "Since when do you spend time with her?"

"I once had a life before I began my indentured fucking servitude here with you." Violet snarls in return.

Brad takes a slow step toward her and I sit up in my seat, Enzo placing a hand out toward me to try and settle me.

"We need to give it a little time, Vin." Enzo chides. He's right and I know it but the anger pulsing through me from the proximity they hold is nearly taking me under.

"I'm sorry Brad. I should have said something." Violet itches at her chest.... at the camera. No, no, no. Brad stares right into me for what seems like an eternity before dragging his gaze back up to her face.

He goes to speak and then his phone rings. "I have to take this. Sit the fuck down." With that he stomps away and through the front door.

"Fuck." Violet says barely above a whisper.

"Don't touch your chest again, Vi. Be cool. Don't try and get anything out of him." I whisper, the message reaching her through the tiny piece tucked in her ear. "Don't respond to me.

I'm right outside, you are safe."

Minutes pass before Brad comes back into the room fully dressed in jeans and a black hooded sweatshirt. "I have business to tend to. I won't be back until morning. You better fucking be here, Violet. I swear to god you won't have legs to run away on again if you aren't."

"I'll be here." She lets out in a monotone breath.

Its going to be a long night.

We watch as Brad pulls out in his gaudy G-wagon. "I wonder if he can sense that he's living his last 24 hours right now?" I ask, smiling at Enzo.

After a hot bath, Violet lays down in her old bed and angles the camera tucked in her shirt at her. I told her she could sleep while Enzo watched the grounds and I watched the camera and the front of the house.

It's currently 4am and there has been no sign of Brad. Enzo is on foot patrolling the area and I've been parked a few houses down watching. Vi hasn't so much as moved a muscle.

The revelation unnerves me. Violet has always had a terrible time sleeping.

I zoom in on Violet and notice that her chest isn't rising or falling anymore.

"Something is up." I speak into the ear piece Enzo is wearing.

"What?" His response is immediate. "No one has came or went. I haven't taken my eyes off this house."

"I'm going in." I'm up and out of the vehicle, moving in before waiting for a response.

"I've got the front." I whisper-yell.

"Back is secure."

I hit the stairs at full speed not bothering with my normal routine of checking doorways and securing rooms. I don't have time for those luxuries if Violet isn't breathing.

I bust into the corner room that once belonged to my wife, where I'm afraid her limp, lifeless body might lay. I don't hesitate nor bother with the door handle before kicking the door down. The wood splinters and dust flies into the air. I scan the bed and then the room quickly.

She's not there.

Her white flowing shirt is draped over the chair in the corner of the room. The camera's still on. The once consistent light now blinking. Someone fucked with the camera without me noticing.

Someone slipped past our security detail.

Violet is missing.

24

Violet

The cold wind whips across my face as something warm and wet drips down my cheek and under my chin. The side of my face is pressed up against a warm hard chest and I fight to keep my eyes open, sleep is awaits just around the corner begging to envelop me.

I nestle my face into Vince as we continue on our journey. "Where are we going now?" I ask.

I'm cold, I'd rather drive. I don't remember this part of the mission we talked about so thoroughly last night. The chest beneath me vibrates with laughter. Ice cold, spurious laughter.

It's not Vincenzo. I try to push up and away but my head throbs with the movement. I notice then that I can barely see straight.

Brad pulls my head back by my hair. "Somewhere we can be alone." His smile is devious and not in the irresistible way Vin's is.

Moments later Brad wrenches open the heavy door of his ridiculous SUV and tosses me into the back seat. "A camera, Violet?" His tone beyond hateful. I can't fathom where he's taking me or what he plans to do to me. "I suppose you probably don't want to start being a good fiancee now and tell me who was on the other end?"

The words turn my stomach sour. I knew I hated this man, I have for years. But the burning repulsion I feel now is unbearable. "Where are you taking me?" I demand, trying to act like all of my power isn't diminished. He doesn't answer as I'm still trying to unblur my vision and breathe through the constant pain in my head. I lift a hand to my face and bring it around in front of me. Bright red blood coats my palm. "Did you fucking hit me?"

"Shut the fuck up or I'll do it again." He throws a silver pistol coated in blood up onto the dash in front of him. This mother fucker pistol whipped me in my sleep. You have got to be shitting me. I glance at the clock on the dash 2:38.

As a matter of fact, where the fuck is Vince? He told me not to worry, he told me to rest, and that I'd be fine. Now I've got a god damn concussion and am stranded with an actual monster. Not the kind the news warns us about, not the kind you think are lurking in the shadows, the kind that hides in plain sight behind a white picket fence.

The kind that makes people disappear without a trace, never to be seen again, without a single consequence or repercussion. The world already thinks I'm missing, it will be nothing to cover up my death.

Brad drives erratically, I'm sure he's got a fresh dose of coke flowing through him. Driving his already elevated rage higher and higher. There seems to be no ceiling with him, his fury is boundless and he has no desire to cap it.

"We can work this out." I plead with him. I can't die today. A far cry from what I felt a month or so ago but I'm not ready now. I've found something else to live for.

The violet's that Vince had planted for me surrounding the house, the foods Noelle was teaching me to cook, the inside jokes with my new brother in law, the beautiful bath tub I'd become enraptured by in the lower level of the castle I called home.

Vincenzo.

I decide in that moment that I will fight. Brad can beat my body down, chastise and belittle me, but he can't touch my soul. That belongs to my husband.

I close my eyes shut tight before I open them once more and sit myself up. I blink a few times to try and steady my vision. Without giving myself time to reconsider I throw an arm over the head rest and around his throat, pulling back with all my might. Sure, I might kill us both with my foolish bravery but at least I'll die trying.

Brad reaches back for my hair and pulls hard, with relentless strength, but I don't let up. I squeeze as tight as I can. The veins in Brad's neck bulge back against me. I can feel spit fly from his mouth as he yells incoherent words at me. I can't listen to that now, I can only hear the steady thrum of my own heart beat in my ears.

He reaches forward and just when I think he's going to jerk the steering wheel hard in an attempt to throw me off he brings his hand back into my face. Hard.

I don't have time to think before the metal collides with my skull once more. I barely register the pain before I'm welcomed by my apparent new favorite color.

Black.

25

Vincenzo

My heart races as I watch the the red blinking dot continue across the Indiana-Kentucky border. We've deduced that they're flying, there's no way they could have traveled by land that fast.

We're moving right behind but we're not quick enough. It's taking every ounce of self control I didn't think I had to stay calm. I have no idea what the fuck he's doing to my angel. The thought turns the blood rushing through me to ice. Before this, I had even considered giving Brad a quick, painless death. He didn't ask for this life, but now that I know he's thoroughly enjoying it I will show him just how much I love my job as well.

A helicopter can't quite keep up with there small plane but we've been in the air longer and we'll be able to land this thing anywhere. Theodore has an office in Memphis, Tennessee, I'm putting all my eggs in one basket by heading straight to the nearest landing spot. I have a car waiting for us and one thing is certain, I won't be leaving without my wife.

"5 minutes." Carlos' voice comes across the headsets we all have on.

He was able to pinpoint a deserted lot big enough for us to land and get to a car I've arranged to be waiting for us. Violet landed 10 minutes ago at the airport and according to my app she is still there now. If we can get to them before they leave, this will be a lot easier and with less casualties.

Carlos stays back with the chopper while Enzo drives us through the city. "Hurry the fuck up!" I shout at him.

"This isn't a fucking Ferrari Vince. We're maxed out!" He yells back. I'm so on edge that I'm almost convinced I could run faster than this fucking car. I notified an acquaintance at the Memphis Police Department of my arrival so we shouldn't have any issues at or around the airport.

"We're going to get her. Don't worry." My brother ensures me as we roll through the gates of the private landing strip. There's a large warehouse to the left and I have a feeling in my gut that's where they are, the app isn't specific enough to show us exact fucking coordinates so intuition will have to do for now.

"Over there." I point to the building and take the gun from my waist, spinning the silencer on and racking it. "No survivors. Brad is mine." That's all I can say before I exit the vehicle and head toward Violet.

Enzo stands on one side of the door and I on the other. Unfortunately from this angle I can't see inside the fogged window but he can. Although he can see more than me, I don't think its much better. I send him a questioning glance but he shakes his head slowly, signifying there are men right on the other side.

I raise my hand and quickly count down on my fingers from three to one. In one swift motion I spin my body to face the door head on and kick it down. I go right while Enzo goes left. Before the guard on my side of the entrance has time to process what's going on I've put a bullet in his head and there's crimson blood leaking from his skull and flowing like a river across the cement flooring.

There's a light coming from under a door 30 yards or so from us and we glide that way with stealth. The door is shut, they must not have heard the commotion from the door falling to the ground. I take my chances and peak into the glass window when I see Brad standing with his shirt off in the center of the room. He's got on a pair of light washed denim jeans and they're soaked in dark blood.

The rage in my body is damn near all-consuming when I let the picture before me sink in. There's no one else that blood would belong to in the circumstance, only Violet.

I look at Enzo and I know the look on my face does the talking I can't. He pauses briefly to pull a hunting knife from the sheath on his back and tosses it to me. My brother knows me so well.

I scan the opposite side of the room and I see my sweet angel tied by thick rope to an old rusted chair in the middle of the room. Her once wheat colored hair is now stained a dark rust color by a steady stream of blood flowing from her head. The pajama top she wore in the video is gone. She's in nothing but her bra and sleep shorts wrapped tightly with a thick silver piece of tape not only covering her mouth but wrapped entirely around her head.

I don't think before I nod to Enzo and it's his turn to free the door from it's hinges. I need every ounce of power to do what I'm about to.

The door goes down and I'm in the room and racing toward Brad at the speed of light. He's a big guy but I'm bigger. He's

quick but I'm quicker.
He's a savage but I'm a fucking nightmare.

26

Violet

My head whips up at the noise behind me. How did Vince find me? The tears I'd refused to shed come out in full force. I've never been so happy to see another human in my life.

"Vin!" I scream but the sound is muffled by the tape over my mouth. I'm barely hanging on to consciousness but the sight of my husband has offered me a small ledge in my mind, so I try and grasp it.

Vincenzo is headed straight for Brad and I begin to panic. I don't know a lot about weapons but I know that Brad is fully armed with not only the gun he's hit me with several times but a handful of other larger ones. I try to scream again but stop the noise from coming out I don't want to distract him. If he really takes a good look at me I know he'll stop what he's doing and come to my aid.

We'd only been in the warehouse for about a half an hour before the door busted down. It only took Brad about 5 minutes to bind me to the cold metal chair. At first he was asking me a series of questions. Did I leave of my own free will? Where was

I? Why was I in such good condition? Who was I working for? Etc. But I refused to answer. At first I stuck with the story of being in Colorado but the fucking psycho called my poor aunt Ali and confirmed that I was indeed lying.

After that I chose to plead the fifth. Unfortunately for me that's when things turned ugly. Every time Brad asked me a question and I didn't answer he took his dull switch blade and raked it slowly across my skin.

Now, I can feel the blood leaking out all over me. In the center of my abdomen, near the top, is the worst. Right under my breasts is the word 'CUNT' engraved into my skin. One letter for a series of 4 questions I was unwilling to answer.

Right before the brothers showed up I was considering my options, I almost told him I was with Vince on the island. The light is currently leaving my vision and I wasn't sure if I could take another incision into my flesh. The one running vertically down the inside of my forearm is draining a steady drip down onto the floor beneath me and the puddle is only getting larger by the minute.

I start to close my eyes and lean my head back when I feel hands on my body and flinch. The last of my energy going into the movement.

"It's just me, V." Enzo's soft voice grounds me back into the moment and I feel a little grin reach my lips. I can feel his swift, leather glove clad hands working rapidly to free me. "Take a deep breath, this is going to hurt."

Fuck, he was right. I think to myself as he rips the tape away from my mouth taking some, maybe all of my hair with it. I barely hear the moan that leaves my mouth.

"Enzo?" I'm not even sure if I was able to say the words out loud. The darkness is ferociously consuming me. I need to get something off my chest before I die, though.

"Tell Vincenzo that I love him."

"No." Enzo's face is hard while he's scooping me into his arms. "You're going to tell him yourself."

These men are impossible.

Back to the abyss I go.

27

Violet

I blink my eyes open trying to fight off the light. The beams are blinding me and the incessant headache I've acquired is unrelenting. I manage to get my eyes all the way open and a scream leaves me before I think better of it.

In front of me Brad hangs from the ceiling by large metal hooks through the thick skin of his back. His head barely moves at the sound of my shriek and blood drips down his body to the floor. I go to stand up and make my way over to him but I'm stopped by large hands on my shoulders.

"*Mio Angelo,* not so fast." I look down to see whats tugging on my hand and notice an IV running fluids and something looking awfully similar to blood into me. "Sit, Violet. You need rest."

"Vince, what's going on?" I can't look away from Brad. I might hate the man but I don't particularly want to see anyone hung by their flesh at any point.

"We are going to get your answers." He smiles a toothy, wicked smile at me. "Mr. Endlow wanted to spill all the details while you were still asleep. We couldn't have that, could we?"

"Let me guess, you drugged him?" I shoot him a disapproving look.

"Am I really that predictable, *Bella Moglie?*" He winks and continues on. "He'll be awake any time now. How are you feeling? The painkillers should still work for a few more hours." I see a flash of anger cross his features but it comes and goes just as fast, before I have time to blink his face has softened and he's staring at me only with adoration.

"I'm fine but Vin, this is a lot.." I trail off as Brad starts to stir. Just as I look up to see if he's fully awake, I see he's staring at me. The look on his face is something like disgust mixed with ungodly pain.

"You fucking bitch." He's barely able to grit the words out between breaths. "Fucking the guy that killed your sister? I knew you were worthless but-" He's cut off by a fist to the ribs from Enzo.

"That's enough of that." Enzo's face is more stern than I've ever seen it before a slow flow of composure washes over it. "No one ever taught you how to speak to a lady?"

"Tell her, Brad. Where were you taking her?" Vince raises and eyebrow as we all wait for his response.

"Fuck you, Bianchi." The smile on Vince's face is eerie. I'd hate to be the one he's aiming his carefully boxed up rage at right now.

"Here's the thing, *Brad,* you can tell Violet where you were taking her and I will give you the courtesy of a quick-ish death or we can play my favorite game. The one where I ask you questions and when you don't answer, I flay the skin from your body piece by fucking piece until your lungs slowly give out and your heart no longer has any blood to pump." Vince takes his blade and wipes both sides on his pants as if he was cleaning it off.

"To my dad, who was going to sell you to some fucking guy in Brazil. Now put a bullet in my brain before I lose my shit." Brad's face is a shade of pale that I've never seen in person on anyone. The sentence is garbled and hard to understand but the words dump over me like a vat of ice water. Sell me?

I know that's what Vince has been telling me for weeks now but to think that was my fate just hours ago. I can't quite wrap my head around it.

"You told your father I was back?" I ask him.

"I thought he took you in the first place and was bullshitting me. You are lucky I let you live. I told you that you'd never get away from me, Violet. In life or death you will never escape me." Brad spits the words like a curse. A chill runs over me as I consider the truth behind them.

Am I ever going to be free of this nightmare? Even if Brad dies here tonight, this experience will stick with me for the rest of my life.

"Did you kill my sister, Brad?" I can't help but cringe a little at the words. I almost don't want to hear his answer. I'm not even sure when exactly I stood up but the situation I've found myself in is overwhelming me and my legs begin to shake. Before my knees give out Vince is behind me lifting me from the ground and setting me back on the bed.

For the first time since I woke up I take a good look around the room. It's definitely got a warehouse feel except much cleaner, sterile almost. There are a few doors with small windows and blinding white lights.

"No you fucking idiot. Not only did I pay your boyfriend to do it but I was with you when it happened." He's got an apparent burst of adrenaline coursing through him as he throws the words at me with venom.

"You were just going to throw me to the wolves? Let your father sell me off to the highest bidder?" My voice grows stronger and more confident as I let my own fury take over. "That means you knew this entire time that your father was buying and selling humans?"

Brad almost laughs at me. "Don't act like your so high and righteous, Violet. Where do you think everything in your possession has come from? Your dad bought his way into the business with your life when you were five fucking years old. Now your fucking a hit man, the same one who put a fucking bullet in your doped out whore of a sister's head. I should be thanking him, I never did want any siblings."

Everything is a blur as I move to Vince and rip the blade away from his hip. I'm in front of Brad the next moment and driving a fistful of metal into his sternum the next. I don't shake, I don't shed a tear, I don't even have to adjust my breathing.

Brad Endlow is dead because of me and it feels damn good.

28

Vincenzo

I stare at Violet in disbelief but I'm so fucking proud of her. The things he was saying to her were worthy of death. Let alone the kidnapping, drugging, and cutting her perfect skin up. These are all triable offenses and no one leaves my court room alive.

Judging by her face I'd say she's in shock. Slowly, I make my way over to her. I put a hand on her shoulder and slide it down to her bicep, then her forearm, before finally sliding my hand over hers and grabbing the blade.

"Take me home." Violets voice is surprisingly normal, if not a bit sleep deprived.

"Enzo, get someone here to clean this up." My eyes don't leave hers as I shout over my shoulder to my brother. I don't mean for the words to come out so harsh but I need to get my girl home and back into our bed as soon as possible.

Enzo is retreating out to the car for his phone when she swiftly turns to face me with her chest pushed up against the top of my stomach. She throws both over warm, sticky hands up around my neck and pull my lips down to meet hers.

The kiss is ridden with need and desperation. There is no gentleness, no love, just pure lust racks through us both as we rip at each others clothes. I lift Violet up into me with two handfuls of her bubble ass.

She brings her right hand down to my chest and I notice that the IV that was helping to sustain her life got ripped out somewhere in the last few minutes and I pull back.

"Violet, you aren't ready for this. You need to rest." I can barely get the words out with my chest heaving so hard. A mix between the adrenaline of hunting them down and now the undeniable need coursing through me.

"Don't tell me what I'm capable of, Vincenzo." Her mouth is back on mine and I'm slamming her spine up against the wall behind the dead man hanging from the ceiling before I know it. Violet is powerful with her tongue, fucking it in and out of my mouth letting her hips follow along. The warmth of her pussy grinding over my cock through my black jeans is driving me insane, I can't have anything else between us.

I set her feet on the ground carefully. "Lay down, Violet." I demand. I can see the blood trailing toward us but it does nothing to deter me from getting inside of my wife.

She lowers herself carefully to the ground without so much as wincing. I know the angle her elbows were bent at strains some of the stitches she received but she doesn't let on if she's feeling any pain.

"Good girl." I praise her after taking my pants off and lowering myself down between her knees.

I'm not careful when I put my hands behind her knees and push them up to her chest. A moan escapes her with the force of the movement and I dive my tongue deep inside of her before swirling it and moving to suck her clit. I repeat the movement over and over until I feel her muscles convulse around me.

Brad's blood has now stained Violet's side and is starting to pool around us. I raise up to my knees and shove my aching cock deep inside her producing a soul shattering scream.

Violet throws her hands flat down onto the concrete splattering the blood on us both. The hot liquid spurs me on more as I fuck her faster and harder. I don't know if I could ever get deep enough inside her.

"Fuck, Vincenzo. More!" She begs and I give it to her. I slow just a little and bring back one knee so I can get deeper. I pump into her deeper, harder, faster until we are nothing but a bloody, blurry mess.

She places her stained hands on the back of my biceps to anchor herself. "I love you, Vince." She cries out, tears stream down her face and I almost halt my movement.

For some reason I always knew she'd get there with me but I wasn't expecting to hear those words in this exact moment. I bend my face next to hers and lick a hot trail of tears into my mouth. "Come, Violet."

That's all it takes.

I can feel her contracting around me while I buck into her, biting and sucking on her anywhere my mouth can reach. It's not long before I'm falling right behind her.

I love you, I think to myself.

But the words never leave my lips.

29

Violet

The light streams through my favorite stained-glass window as the sun stands tall and proud in the blue sky. It's the deceiving type of beam that makes you think it's warm outside but in reality the wind actually hurts your face.

I hear the steady beep of the monitors I'm hooked up to on my side of the bed. I'm done with the blood but because I haven't been able to stay conscious long enough to eat or drink anything I've still got fluids running.

It's been a few days since we got back to the island and today my appetite is insatiable but I'm not talking about food. I carefully roll over to stroke a hand down Vince's solid body but he's not there. I let out an exasperated sigh and rub my palms down my face.

"Right here, *Mio Amore*." Vince smiles at me from the bathroom door. He's standing there shirtless in his sweats, the v-line of his abdomen almost like an arrow pointing to his hard, thick co-

Vince laughs. "Well good morning to you too, wife. If I didn't know any better I'd say you're objectifying me right now." He crosses the room to the door and scans his finger over the metal box.

"Wait, where are you going?" When did I become one of those girls? Yuck.

Vince chuckles again. "Just opening the door ahead of time so I can carry you through."

Vince walks back over to me and unhooks me from the IV. "Dr. Partello said we could discontinue the fluids today if you can eat breakfast and keep it down."

Thank God, I'm so tired of worrying about the damn tube getting ripped out. Again. I want to move without reservation and sleep with my arm under my pillow again.

Vince slides a hand behind my back and under my thighs to lift me into his chest. I wince at the way he has me bent. My new tattoo creasing in an uncomfortable way.

When I woke up wrapped in familiar black satin sheets a few days ago I had a peculiar burning sensation under my breasts. I looked down to see that the word Brad carved into me was replaced with beautiful angel wings, dark and almost decrepit, but beautiful nonetheless. While I don't exactly remember to consenting to such a thing I can't deny that it made me smile. I wasn't particularly fond of the word under it or the memory, so to see it replaced with something beautiful and unique to me, us even, was refreshing.

The wings of an angel, fallen and caught by a demon.

Downstairs Noelle greets us with a smorgasbord of different breakfast items. There is everything ranging from donuts to bacon, waffles and crepes. The woman didn't spare a single item for my first breakfast since we left a week ago.

"Noelle! Are you serious? You must of been working on this for hours!" I'm uncomfortable with the gesture, I'm not used to a caring mother figure in my life.

"A simple 'thank you' would do, Mrs. Bianchi." She raises an eyebrow at me and waves a hand for Vince to set me in the chair next to hers.

"I'm sorry.. I'm so happy to see you!" We've been back a few days and while I was lucid for some moments I mostly slept, Vince wouldn't let me leave the room. In fact, he's been acting kind of strange since we've been back. "Donuts *and* bacon?! You've outdone yourself once again." I give her my most sincere smile and for once that's exactly what it is, sincere.

I turn to my husband and frown at the sight. His eyes seem a bit sunken and there are dark circles lining them. "What's wrong?" I ask him.

"Nothing." He gives me a small smile that's anything but sincere.

I rest my hand on his muscular thigh. God, I love these thighs. "Vincenzo." I give him a serious look. "Tell me what's wrong."

"It's good to see you eating again, *Mio Amore*."

"Then smile, Vin." I lift my hand from his leg and press my palm against his cheek. "I'm fine, thanks to you."

"It's not thanks to me, Violet. I put you in that position in the first place." His voice is loud as he stands abruptly from the chair leaving my hand suspended in midair.

"I'm leaving today. I'll be gone a few days." I'm having a hard time reconciling the loving man I've spent the last few days with and the man in front me now. "Noelle and Matteo will be here to help."

"Where are you going?" I ask. I know Vince hasn't been working but I'm not sure that he really needs to.

"I don't answer to you, Violet." He turns and leaves the kitchen and heads back upstairs.

I look to Noelle, confused, but she just lowers her head and shakes it slowly.

"Vincenzo doesn't know how to show affection, Violet. Don't take it personally. He's taking your-" She pauses looking for a suitable word for the torture I withstood almost a week ago. "*Injuries* very personal."

I don't have time to argue the stupidity of that statement. I scoff at the term "affection", he's certainly shown me he knows how to be affectionate. There is nothing that he could have done differently to change the outcome of our trip back home. At the end of the day he found me, helped me, and the problem has been rectified.

I run after after Vince. "Wait, Vin. Talk to me!"

I catch up to him but he doesn't respond, he doesn't even turn to face me.

"Vincenzo!" I'm too close to yell his name, but I do it anyways. I won't be ignored. Not by him.

He turns and grabs my shoulders, throwing me up against the wall. Vince winces at the small gasp that leaves me and drops my shoulders.

"Are you going back?" I don't specify where, he knows what I mean.

Vince lowers his face down to mine so we are eye level, like he's speaking to a child. "It's none of your damn business what I'm doing. I won't tell you that again."

"I want to go with you. I still don't know what happened to my sister." My voice is strong, I'm determined to win this argument. He knows how important it is to me.

"Absolutely not. Theodore is going to be looking for his son and I will not have you caught in the cross hairs. You know that he told his father that he was delivering you to him, he knows you were the last person to see Brad." His eyes and tone are stern. His voice doesn't waver as his chest rises and falls steadily.

He stares deep into my eyes. "You won't be victim to any other man but me again, *Mio Angelo*."

His arms are on both sides of my head now and the heat forming between us is unsettling. Just when I think he's going to lean in to kiss me he pushes off the wall and backs away. He walks down the hall and scans his finger to gain entrance to his office. He doesn't spare me a second glance before entering and slamming the door closed.

30

Vincenzo

I've located Theodore and he's back in Michigan. I'm sure looking for his precious son. However, Brad is currently in over a thousand pieces. Flushed down various drains and pipes so that won't be happening anytime soon.

I'm still not sure how I plan to have him confess to murdering his 18 year old mistress. I wouldn't say he's a big component for honesty and I don't think he'll be moved by Violet's emotions either. Not that I'd bring her with me again.

I'm still fucking kicking myself for bringing her on a mission. I let my feelings get in the way and allowed her to get hurt, that won't be happening again.

Right on cue there's obnoxious banging on the door. When we got back to the island I removed her fingerprint access from all doors but our bedroom. "Vincenzo! Open this damn door!" I can't help the smile forming on my face, she's so damn cute when she's mad.

"I'm working." I answer back as I walk toward the door to open it. I just wanted to rile her up a bit more.

"Vince, I swear to God if you don't open this door I'll-" I open the door swiftly, cutting her off.

"You'll what, my delicate little flower? Stab me to death?" Her swallow is audible at my choice of words. "Surely a little blood wasn't too much for you, Vi?" I know I'm being an asshole but she needs to understand that she can't come back with me. That douche bag was only one of many people who will die a slow, bloody death at my hand.

"Fuck you, Vince." She starts to turn her body and walk away but I can't stop myself from grabbing a fist full of my favorite long blonde hair. She whimpers at my force and it only spurs me on.

"Running now, *Amore Mio?* We're just getting started." I know the smile on my face is anything but welcoming as I drag her into my office and throw her down on the ground.

"Take your clothes off, Violet." It's not a question but a demand.

She doesn't argue as she sits up and slowly pulls off her sleep set, already naked underneath. Her nipples are hard, her chest heaving as I walk over to her. "Good girl."

I step over her to my desk and grab some zip ties out of the drawer. I pull my high back leather chair around to the front and then pick up Violet to set her in it. I don't let her get comfortable before I tie each wrist to an arm of the chair. "What the fuck, Vin?" She's pissed but I notice the way she rubs her thighs together, the subtle pink hue taking over her exposed chest.

"You're right, this won't work." I walk out of my office and take my time walking down to the pole barn where I grab some duct tape. Violet won't move. Not only is she naked and tied to the chair, but she knows better.

On my way back to the office I stop by our room and grab

my belt. Violet is just where I expected her to be, in the chair in the middle of the room soaking wet and pissed.

I rip a piece of the tape off and slap it down on her mouth before she has the time to question me. Then I take the thick belt and buckle it around her waist so she's unable to move her body.

"There we go." I step back and admire my work. "I wish you could see yourself, Violet. You look fucking beautiful right now." Her cheeks redden a bit at my words and she looks down at my painful erection. I mean it, she looks so gorgeous with her luscious locks, beautiful porcelain skin, and the tarnished angel wings beneath her breasts.

"Do you have any idea how long I've been waiting to taste you, wife?" Slowly I lower myself down to my knees. I bite down on the inside of her thigh and she cries out into the tape while bucking her hips up. "So impatient." I meet her striking silvery eyes and smile up at her. They're pleading as I lick and bite at her inner thighs for the better part of 10 minutes. There's a puddle under her in my work chair and I couldn't be more thrilled that my office will smell a little more like her now.

"Open your legs as wide as you can Violet." My face is serious now and I mean exactly what I'm about to say. "If you move at all while I eat your pussy I will stop and have Noelle come up here and untie you, got it?"

She shivers and goose bumps cover her skin but she just stares wide-eyed at me. "You got it?" I yell up at her.

She shakes her head yes and I pounce. I shove my tongue as deep as I can into Violet's sopping hole. I fuck her with my tongue until she's screaming into her tape. I only stop to look at my beautiful wife's face. "You're such a good girl, Vi. You listen so well."

A tear runs down her cheek as she watches me move back to her pussy. I flatten my tongue before moving up and down on her clit a few times and then suck it into my mouth hard. I suck a few more times before shoving two fingers inside of her. Only a few thrusts and she's coming all over my face. I groan into her egging her on with the vibrations.

When I'm sure the orgasm is gone I sit up and rip the tape from her mouth. I kiss her deep, fucking her mouth the same way I just did her pussy and she moans into me. Still desperately trying to buck her hips up looking for relief. "What do you need, Violet?"

"You. I need you!" She barely gets the words out in her haze of lust.

"No, tell me exactly what you fucking need." I keep my voice calm but stern. It's almost impossible not to rip my pants down and sink into her but I have to hear her beg. The need radiating off of her, amping us both up is worth the wait.

"Please, Vin. Fuck me." She throws her head back and moves her hips in the chair trying to create some type of friction.

Quickly, I undo the belt from around her waist and pull her ass to the edge of the chair. I leave her there for just a moment to pull my joggers down.

I place one hand around her throat and the other behind her right knee, lining myself up with her "You want my cock, Violet?"

"Yes, Vincenzo. I want your cock, please!" She begs and that's all I need to fucking hear.

Reluctantly, I inch myself in slower than usual since it's been a few days and she was, well, incapacitated for a couple of those days.

I bottom out and then pull up to the tip before slamming back down into her. I do it again and again, hard but slow, trying to keep us from moving to much in the rolling chair.

"Fuck me, Vince." Violet moans loudly.

I pick up my pace and she meets me thrust for thrust. The chair slams into the solid oak desk but I don't let up. I drill into her until I'm panting and have felt her convulse around my hard cock at least two more times.

I lean over to bite down hard on Violet's neck and she screams out. I suck the spot into my mouth before I press up on both hands to look at her. "You are everything, Violet."

"I love you." She whispers back to me.

After I finish, I untie Violet and take her back to our room.

I can figure my plan out tomorrow.

Once I'm sure Violet is asleep for the night I sneak out from underneath her and make my way down to my office. I may or may not have snuck some sleeping pills into her water.

I make myself comfortable at my desk and then turn on the camera in our bedroom. Violet hasn't moved an inch. Her sweet face rests on her forearm and her face is toward the camera. I stare for a bit before turning on my work laptop and logging in.

I've been watching Theodore's communications more frequently since we got back from our last trip. Unfortunately, he's been watching the incoming and outgoing flights like a hawk. I'm not sure if Brad told him he was in communication with me but the last thing I need is for him to notice my flight pattern aligning with his son's failure to appear. I also can't have Carlos fly us in without notifying the towers and risk having us shot down.

Plan B is to take the yacht. Not my favorite mode of

transportation in late fall, not only is it cold but entirely to flashy for me. However, I know there's a private beach that I can anchor down at and take the life boat up to shore without being seen.

I'll spend the rest of the day with Violet tomorrow and then I'll get the guys together to leave at midnight.

I guess one more night of a sound sleep won't hurt her.

31

Violet

Three times.

Three times this morning Vincenzo stepped away from me and out of the kitchen to take phone calls.

Not that Vin and I have spent 30 years together or anything but he doesn't usually mind my presence when it comes to his work affairs. I know what he does for a living and while it's not a path I'd choose for myself or a loved one, I accept it nonetheless.

Which leaves me thinking, is this a work call? I can't sneak out of the kitchen now to eaves drop, that's too noticeable. I'll wait for him to pad his way down to his office and see if I can hear him threw the door.

"*Mio Amore*, what shall we do today?" Vince strides back through the door beaming before leaning down to plant a slow but firm kiss on my forehead.

"I'm feeling a bit groggy today, actually. I was thinking a lazy day. Maybe read a little or bake with Noelle." All of those things sounds wonderful and while I do feel a bit hungover today even though I haven't drank, those things are far from my true intent.

VIOLET

I want Vince to think I'm busy so he will let his guard down, maybe let something slip or stand somewhere less secluded than he thinks so I can figure out why he's being so secretive.

He has no reason to lie to me and my gut feeling isn't typically wrong so I'm going to ride this out and see where it takes me.

"I've been craving Noelle's pumpkin cheesecake muffins." He practically moans trying to form his words. I've noticed my husband has a sweet tooth.

"I love pumpkin!" I don't. "Muffins and iced coffee are my favorite."

"Really? I seem to recall you despising pumpkin, actually." Vince raises an eyebrow at me and crosses his arms over his chest. Shit, I forgot he's a literal stalker. He also knows I wouldn't say that just to make him happy. Mentally, I scramble for a second trying to formulate a good lie.

I force a laugh. "Okay well I do love muffins and iced coffee, maybe we'll make two flavors." I wink at Vin and he only glares back unfazed at my attempt to be cute.

"Keep an eye on my *piccolo imbroglione*, Noelle." He gives her a stern look before leaving the room, without so much as a see you later for me.

After Vince is gone I ask, "What does *piccolo imbroglione* mean?"

"You'll have to ask Vincenzo, Mrs. Bianchi." Noelle shoots me a smug grin knowing that I hate when she is so formal with me.

"Whatever." I roll my eyes. "Do you think we could make snicker doodle muffins?" I fight the urge to say never mind. They're my favorite. My grandma and I used to make them every year around the holidays before she passed away when I was 9. It was the only seasonal tradition I've ever had.

"I haven't made them before but I'm sure we could muster a recipe up." Her smile now is genuine and I return one of my own.

Noelle and I spend the next several hours talking about her life and childhood in Italy. For those few hours I let myself feel like I belong to a family, that I might some day make my own traditions with this band of criminals I've come to know and love.

Sometime after lunch I sneak up to my room and do some reading in the custom corner that I discovered Vincenzo made just for me. I wrap up in a soft fleece blanket for a bit with something spooky, spicy, and magical before my curiosity gets the best of me.

I set the book down on the blanket I tossed over the ottoman and head for the door. I'm careful to be quiet but not unnervingly quiet. If I'm caught by anyone I don't want them to think I'm acting weird.

I creep down the hallway and stop at the door in front of Vin's office. At first I consider scanning my finger but I can't remember if he can tell or not if attempts are made so, I refrain. Plus, I'm not really looking to speak with him at the moment. I lean into the door and press my ear up to it tight. I don't hear anything and after about thirsty seconds I start to lean up when I hear him answer his cell.

"Coordinates?" Vin's loud voice is perfectly clear through the thick door.

"Okay it will be approximately three and a half hours form shore to shore."

"Yes."

"I will see you then."

Loud foot steps boom toward the door and I take off for my room like my life depends on it. At this point, who knows.

I race down the hall and into my room leaving the door open. I just curl up in the chair with the blanket and book when I hear more footsteps right outside of my door way.

"Good book, wife?" I look up to meet dark green eyes burning into my soul.

"Yes." Is all I can reply back. I'm trying to be careful with my words. I don't want him to think I'm being too short or too defensive. I'm not sure I can really win right now.

"What's it about?" His stare is unwavering. I fight the urge to look away but ultimately cave.

"Same old, same old." I lower my eyes down to the book and flip the page. "Fairies, fighting, fucking, all the good stuff." I look back up and wink feeling a little more comfortable in my lie now.

"Hm." He pauses and looks me up and down. His stare hovers over the scars running up my forearms before looking away and heading back out the door. "Noelle will be making pizzas tonight, I thought we could help her." He pauses and looks down for a moment. "If you're feeling up to it?"

I hate that Vince blames himself for what happened. I was literally wearing a body camera and mic there's nothing else he could have done that would have been more protective. Brad was a horrible person, he did horrible things to people for fun. Luckily, Vin was there to save me from him or who knows what would have happened. I brush the thought off because it's pointless to even ponder it. He's dead and he won't hurt me or anyone else ever again.

"I'd love that." I start to stand to walk to my husband but he stops me.

"Rest, *Mio Angelo*. I have some business to tend to, I will find you later." He gives me one more once over and leaves the room.

If he wouldn't have fucked me into oblivion yesterday I'd think he was scared of me.

I sit back for a few minutes until I hear the front door unlatch and then close again. I walk to the small window leading to the back of the house, or maybe the front, I guess it depends if you'd call the beach or the door and driveway the front. I like the beach best.

Vincenzo strides down to the pole barn where Enzo waits for him in his own side by side. I'm not sure what they are up to but they are *not* leaving me out.

32

Vincenzo

I never knew how much I needed Violet.
    I knew I had to have her when I saw her. I knew she'd be my wife and have my children. What I didn't know was that watching her befriend my housekeeper would heal me in ways that I didn't know I needed or that I'd start looking for the lingering scent of her in every room I went in to. I had no idea she'd envelop me in every aspect of her life. I would think I was drowning if it didn't feel so good.
    Regrettably, I'm still an asshole. The thoughts swirling in the back of my brain about the love I have for my wife and the life I've built on my island are quiet compared to my need to keep her safe.
    I continue my way up the stairs with a glass full of water and enough medication to put a small whale to sleep for a few days. That's exactly what I need, a few days. I know that she won't sleep that long but I'll be elbow deep in the remaining Endlow's intestines by then.
    Noelle is privy to my escapades and knows her role here in caring for Violet. I'm somewhat of an apothecary genius when

it comes to incapacitating others. It's certainly come in handy over the years.

Quickly, I scan my finger and bust through the door of our bedroom. Violet is already tucked into the satin black sheets in nothing but a tank top and thong. The contrast of her milky white skin and honey hair against my dark sheets sends a bolt of electricity straight to my dick.

Her eyes are heavy, my girl is already tired. I smirk at the thought of the next hour. It's already 10:00 but after she drinks this glass she'll be so out of it, practically paralyzed, I could do anything to her and she wouldn't wake up.

I reach down to adjust myself. The black jeans I'm wearing do absolutely nothing to hide the erection I'm sporting. I could change into something comfier but I'll be able to leave in thirty minutes and I don't have time for it.

"Drink, *Bella Moglie*. We must keep you hydrated." I pass her the glass and she brings it to her lips. "Good girl". I grab her bottom jaw and lean down to kiss her.

Walking over to the bathroom I close the door and shoot a text to Enzo letting him know I'll be down in the barn at 23:00 to get things around for the trip. We got a lot around yesterday but I want to be loaded and ready by midnight.

Carlos isn't going to come this time. I'm having him stay back to help Matteo with security while I'm gone. I refuse to be negligent with my wife again.

After a brief exchange with my brother I head back to find the water gone and Vi sound asleep, stretched across the bed with her mouth open and soft breaths falling out. I squat down in front of her face and trace the out line of her brow, then her cheek, until I reach her mouth and add a second finger. Pressing in just a little I run the pads of my fingers over her warm tongue and she close her mouth around them out of reflex.

I glance down at my watch hoping the time has changed miraculously. It hasn't. I close my eyes and take a deep breath in. Standing up I head for the door.

I haven't left yet and I'm already counting down the minutes until I'm back inside my room, back inside of her.

"The boat's running. Carlos and I loaded everything. We just need to grab something to carry and we can go." Enzo stands in the pole barn gesturing down to the arsenal I keep in the cellar. I know he's probably carrying at his back, hip, and maybe even leg. He's got quite the obsession with firearms.

I walk to the wall and grab a simple AR-15 and call it good. Between the pistol in my back, the knife on my chest and the stuff I've got on the boat this should be enough.

"Let's go." I turn and head up the stairs to the main door. The blood rushing through me feels like a foreign glowing, hazardous source fueling me.

The thought of ending the man who tore my family apart is so enticing that I'll have to remind myself to drag it out, I need information for Violet as well.

I won't let Theodore Endlow leave this earth until he's repented for his sins, all of them.

33

Violet

My blood boils as I sit up and watch Vincenzo pad down the driveway to his stupid garage. Does he not know that you can't just go around drugging people? If I confront him he'll say it's for my own good or some other oppressive argument I'm just really not in the mood to hear.

The man is insufferable. He'd never accept my insistence that he's being an asshole by continually drugging me. I had a hunch but today when I pretended to drink the water I swear his eyes actually twinkled as he watched me "sip" it. I only raised it to my lips to see what kind of reaction I'd receive, he failed.

I rush down the hall to my room and change into an all black ensemble. Thick black leggings, black long sleeve tee and sweatshirt, followed by a puffy vest and cute woven hat. The autumn air is crisp and I don't have time to be cold as I stalk my husband and brother in law through the woods tonight.

I try and fail to quietly slide through the front door. My finger print isn't working and I know he did it on purpose. I take a deep breath and regroup. The door in the kitchen leading out to the patio on the beach is rarely locked.

I make my way over to it before I'm greeted by the faint smell of menthol cigarette smoke. I don't think much of it as I quietly slide the glass door open and step one foot through, trying not to shriek in excitement.

"Not so fast, Mrs. Bianchi." Noelle sits at the kitchen island stubbing out her lit cigarette. I've never seen the woman smoke one single time.

"I'm just getting some fresh air. I was having a hard time slee-" She cuts me off before I can lie any further.

"You haven't had any trouble sleeping after your homemade 'Vincenzo Cocktail' any other night?" She slides her chair out and walks toward me. "It's almost like you didn't even drink it?" Noelle stops in front of me, looking me up and down, and I can't help myself from feeling a little afraid. Her look is stern and her tone is anything but adoring.

I decide now is a good time to quit lying. "I didn't drink it and shame on you for condoning that." I put my hands on my hips for a second but I quickly lower them when I start to feel like a scolded child.

Noelle walks right past me like I'm not standing directly in front of her. She opens a heavy drawer near the floor over to the far right of the kitchen. The doors above it hold things we never use when we bake or cook together, so I don't spend much time over there.

She moves some things around and then heads back my way. The light is dim but when she's right in front of me my eyes widen.

"Open your legs." I don't hesitate. Noelle places a leather strap around my thigh. "I know you know how to use a knife. You can have mine." She holds out a large dagger-looking object to me. There are roses and entangled vines engraved into the sides of the hilt with a long, sharp black blade. I meet Noelle's eyes and she has that familiar smile that I love so much.

"Our histories are not the same, Violet. But this knife will keep you safe just as well." Noelle grabs my face and kisses my cheek. "The captain is departing at midnight." She winks and strides out of the room.

Of course she won't tell me where to find him, nor will she stop me, she'll give a me riddle to solve and wish me the best. I tuck the blade into the holster at my thigh and leave.

I'm up and on my feet siding through patio door as quick as I can. I round the side of the castle to head toward the long driveway. I run at top speed all while trying to be mindful of my footsteps on the pavement. There are no lights, no sounds, nothing to follow.

I'm banking on the yacht and I'll be screwed if they're taking something else. I don't remember exactly where the dock is, we've only been by it a few times but I know it's closer to Enzo's side of the island than ours. So, I head that way. It's at least 15 minutes from where I stand now and that's if I run as fast as I can with no breaks.

I don't take anymore time to think about it before I take off. I make sure to be cautious of my surroundings as I sprint through the woods, I'm not sure if there are truly bears and wolves here as Vince said but I don't want to find out. All I have is my knife and I definitely don't want to be in that close of proximity to have to defend my self with it.

I slow my steps as I hear the low murmur of what I'm assuming to be my husband and his men talking. I try to slow my breathing and strain my ears to listen for any coherent words but it's no use.

I peak out of the bush I've hidden behind and see the giant boat has started to leave the dock. With only seconds to spare, I raise to my full height and run like I've never run before. I jump over logs and through mud to the dock. It takes every last ounce of energy I have to launch my self from the dock to the back ledge of the boat.

My footing almost falters as I catapult myself through the air and land with a hard thud on the wooden deck. My knees ache already but I shake it off and sit myself up.

As soon as I sit up hazel eyes meet mine. My body pauses in terror at being caught, after all the hard work I've put in they'll have to physically restrain me to make me stay here on this island.

Enzo smiles and takes the joint from his mouth. "Nothing, some ropes fell." He yells out and then wiggles his fingers at me in a 'hello' gesture.

I smile back.

These people are certifiable, I love it.

After Enzo makes his way back to where ever he came from I make my way into the small storage room in the back where he once stood. I curl up in the corner and let my eyes close for just a moment. I haven't been to the gym in weeks, maybe months now, and my near death experience kind of took it out of me.

Once I feel the boat halt and the steady thrum of the motor ceases, my eyes jolt open. We must have made it to shore. I lift onto my knees to peek into the next room over but don't see anything.

Crawling on my hands and knees I make my way through that door way and into another dark room lined with windows. I head for the right side of the room, closest to the water, and slowly rise back up on to my feet to look through.

Outside Vince is lowering a small metal boat down to the water.

Shit.

Of course he couldn't pull this damn thing right up to the shore it would get stuck. I sink down on bent knees and weigh out my options. I can either jump in and swim to shore or come clean and ride over on the boat with him. The water will be freezing and I have no idea how far we are from shore but I don't know if he'll let me come with him.

This is probably exactly why Enzo let me come, he knew I'd never be able to get away with it.

Dick.

I suppose I could also look for some other type of life boat or floating device to get to shore but then what? There's no way to tell exactly where we are and I surely don't have a vehicle parked and waiting like I'm betting Vin does.

I inhale a deep breath and stand to my full height. I march over to where my husband is letting the boat down and slide an arm around his waist in an attempt to be cute or maybe funny, I don't know. I wasn't counting on this part. I sure as fuck wasn't counting on the elbow that flies into my stomach knocking the wind out of me as a I hit the wooden floor.

Hard.

"Fuck, Violet! I could have killed you!" Vince lowers himself down to scoop me up. "Are you okay? Why are you out here?" His eyes flicker back and forth between mine. They are soft but I can tell he's irritated.

"I'm fine, Vin. I might have a little bruise tomorrow but I'm fine. Put me down." I wiggle my butt in his arms but he only holds on tighter.

"I said why the fuck are you out here?" All the softness from when he thought for a split second that I was injured is gone. "You're going back." He sets me on his feet and heads to the front of the boat.

"No, I'm not Vincenzo." I plead with him. "You are not doing this without me."

He turns to face me. "How do you know I'm not headed out for work?" He steps toward me now. "How do you know I'm not on my way to kill some helpless 18 year old girl right now?"

He's trying to scare me but it won't work. I trust this man with my life. I trust him more than anyone I've ever met, including Victoria. That thought hurts a little bit as it registers but I push the feeling to the side. I don't have time to process those types of emotions right now.

"If you were 'working' you wouldn't have hid it from me. You wouldn't have tried to drug me. Don't lie to me Vince, I've been lied to enough in my life, don't be like them."

I hardly have time to suck in a breath before his hand shoots out and squeezes tight around my throat. "Do not compare me to any of the fucking idiots who sold, bought, or birthed you ever again." I didn't even realize it was possible but he squeezes tighter. My vision blackens around the edges. "Do you understand me, *wife?*" He says the word as if it's a threat.

I try and nod my head but the force of his grip is unrelenting. He leans his face into mine and kisses my open mouth before letting me go.

"I should strip you and tie you up to wait for me upstairs in my bed." I shudder at his words. He's turned me into a monster.

"But you would like that too much, wouldn't you, *Mio Angelo?*" I rub my thighs together desperate for a little friction, a little relief. His calloused and strong, tattooed hands have become my new favorite necklace. His voice like honey soothing the throat he made sore.

"Please, Vincenzo." I can't be certain what I'm begging for right now, so I'll let him decide.

"This is your last trip back to St. Lane's. You will get your answers tonight and we won't have this conversation again. Ever." He doesn't ask if I understand this time because he doesn't care if I do or don't. His gaze is full of malice and lust.

Two more things of his that have also become favorites of mine.

34

Vincenzo

Enzo tries to hide a smug smile as he glances at Violet and I. "You motherfucker!" I stop spinning the wheel to raise the boat and rush him. "You knew."

"Vin, stop!" I barely hear the words. I swing on Enzo but he dodges my first hit. I swing again and catch him in the stomach.

"Did you help her?" I swear that one of these days he's going to piss me off for the last time.

"Of course not, big brother." He winks at me and if it weren't for my wife standing behind me screaming at me to chill the fuck out I would throw him into the freezing cold water below us.

"If something happens to my wife while we're out, you won't make it back." I step back to the wheel and continue bringing the boat up to us.

Violet stands to my left hugging her arms around her waist trying to keep warm. She's got warm clothes on but the breeze from the lake is intense. Aside from tracking Theodore down and playing my own fucked up version of Sunday confessional, I haven't thought about my steps further.

The Woodruff family is far from free of guilt in the circumstances Violet has found her self in but I'm not sure how she'll feel about me murdering her parents, let alone while she's with me. I guess we'll have to cross that bridge when we get to it.

"In." I reach my hand out for Vi to take, while helping her step into the boat. "Good girl, sit down."

I step into the boat next leaving Enzo no choice but to have to burn the fuck out of his hands on the rope as he slowly descends us the rest of the way down to the water. He shoots a glare at me to which I return with a kiss. I guess he's not in the mood to joke now.

The ride from the yacht up to the shore where I had ATV's left takes about 40 minutes. Violet's cheeks and nose are bright red and I can see that she's clearly tired. As much as I hate that she's here, I love her ferocity, her drive and ambition. It's an effort to remember everything that infuriates me about her is also what attracted to me her in the first place.

When I first laid eyes on Violet I could see that she was wild under the surface. A feral power was busting at her seams to be unleashed after being pushed down for so long. While I want to keep her safe, I also want her to thrive.

Violet and I will rule this fucking world together.

We reach the shore and embark on a quick 10 minute or so walk along the rocky, wooded shore line. There are two X-Pro's waiting for us in an alcove away from the water.

"Follow me." I tell Enzo while handing Violet the helmet that was placed on the seat.

"Yes, your majesty." He replies with a bow. I can't stand the guy. Violet laughs and I glare down at her while I buckle the clasp under her chin extra tight.

She turns to throw a leg over the four wheeler and I give her ass a hard slap. "Don't provoke him, Vi."

We're off in a matter of seconds, speeding through the woods. The quads are extra quiet, just the way I like them. Silent but deadly as we make our way to the Tahoe waiting for us at the edge of the woods.

Stepping up into the drivers seat I realize it's already 4 in the morning and it'll be another hour and a half before we make it to the office Theodore will be working in today. Enzo slides into the seat next to me and Violet leans over the council into the front seat.

"Where next?" It appears she's gotten her second wind as she smiles up at us fro her perch in the back.

"Get some sleep, *Mio Amore*. We're going to visit some bad people today."

Violet's soft snores fill the car and suddenly I'm not so pissed she tagged along. I would have been distracted checking the cameras repeatedly had she stayed anyway. Maybe it was for the best or maybe I'll be more distracted keeping an eye on her, I guess only time will tell.

"There he is." Enzo snaps his gaze in the direction of mine. Together we watch Theodore exit his car in the dark parking garage, completely unsuspecting. He must not know that arrogant men bleed just the same.

Quickly and quietly we slide out of the SUV and I lock Violet in. Enzo and I make brief eye contact behind the car to time our movements. This is far from the first time we nabbed someone from a parking garage, we know what to do.

Enzo and I not only work well together but our movements are sometimes so in tune that I can't tell where he starts and I stop. We can take a man down in 3 seconds flat without a single weapon. We can track someone like a dog and put a bullet between their eyes before they've even realized they pissed someone off. It's nothing for us to throw the Rohypnol filled bag over his head, tie it tight around his throat with a rope, and cuff him.

It hardly takes us 5 minutes to complete the task and throw him in the truck. Theodore is no small man, he's kept up on his physique over the years. I can tell he's been in the gym by the solidity of his body as we hoist him up. I let his head slam into the floor. Violet doesn't even stir at the commotion. Only when I'm back in the drivers seat, out of the parking garage, and headed down the road does she sit up and stretch her arms up over her head.

"Good morning, *Bella Ragazza.*" I smirk at her through the rear view mirror as she rubs her eyes. "Are you hungry?"

"Yes! I have been dying for some fast food." She beams back up at me, genuinely excited for the artificial garbage. "Don't roll your eyes at me, Vin. You can't tell me you don't crave some fried hash browns and a fountain pop every once in a while."

Her eyebrow is raised and I know if we were standing outside she'd have her little hand on a popped hip ready to argue about any and everything. While I don't ever crave fast food I do crave her and it's the least I can do to oblige her.

I pull into the nearest drive thru and she orders one of damn near everything. Before I know it were passing things around, sharing, and taking bites of each others food. Something that Enzo and I have never engaged in. While we are all each other have in the formal sense we don't do things like this. We rely on one another, we keep each other alive.

Until there's a low moan in the back seat and the chatter

dies down. Violet scrunches her brow and looks around, I can tell she's questioning whether she heard something or not. Theodore moans again but a bit louder this time. Violet jumps up and looks in the backseat. A piercing scream rings through the car.

"What the fuck, Vince?" She looks between me and the back seat frantically. "Is that Theo?"

"Sit down, Vi." Now I'm remembering why I didn't want her here. Yeah, maybe she's a bit wild and dark. Maybe she killed someone a week ago but to me she's pure. Innocent and clean, only dirtied against her will by the vile family figures in her life.

It's one thing for her to know what I do, it's another for her to watch. Nevertheless, here we are and it must be done. She's still on her knee looking back into the trunk, then to Enzo and I.

"I said sit the fuck down, Violet." I don't raise my voice but it's somber and she knows I'm not playing. She lowers herself down and puts her seat belt back on.

We drive in silence the rest of the way back to the Endlow's house.

35

Violet

We sit at their family dining table like I have a thousand times in my life. As a child, a young girl, and a eventually a woman. I've shared laughter and jokes at this table the same as I've shared heartbreak and tears.

I hate this house.

The good memories are far overshadowed by the bad. The familiar scent of orange and clove twisting my stomach the longer I inhale.

Ana, the sweet young girl who has been cleaning the residence for the last two years, has bruises running up her arms to her throat. Her eyes are sunken and she looks like she's lost even more weight. We've got to be about the same age and were inducted into this piss poor excuse for a family around the same time.

"We aren't going to hurt you, Ana." I wipe the tear falling from her eye since her hands are restrained behind her back. "We're here to take care of a few things and then we're going to send you back to your family in Germany, okay?"

She nods her head back in response but the look in her eyes

tells me she doesn't believe me. I don't waste time making promises to her, I know that I mean it. Actions are a hell of a lot more convincing than being pacified by pretty words and hope. Girls like us learn not to be deceived by such a thing. Hope is crushing, lethal.

"I wanted to make sure you were comfortable, I'm going to go back downstairs for a little bit but then I'll be back. Just try and be quiet, it won't be long." I tuck a strand of her beautiful cinnamon hair behind her ear and stand from the squatting position I was in.

I turn to leave the room but stop as she speaks. "Be careful, Ms. Woodruff."

"Were friends Ana, just call me Violet." I muster up a warm smile hoping to bring her a little peace in the hellish moment she's found herself in.

"Be careful, Violet." She doesn't smile back,

Once I reach the bottom of the basement stairs it doesn't take me long to find the men. I follow the sound of a metal baseball bat tapping on the cement floor.

I've been in this basement countless times but only one half of it. The half that consists of leather reclining couches, foosball tables, and giant flat screen televisions mounted every where.

I've never been to this side.

It's dark and damp with concrete flooring and a hallway consisting of what looks like jail cells lining both sides of the walls. Aside from the site being absolutely atrocious, the first thing that pops into my mind is that they all know. His wife, Brad, the people employed in this home all must know that Theodore Endlow brings girls and women down here into this house of horrors to be raped, beaten, and sold off to the highest bidder.

Vince told me that my mother was too obsessed with the way she lived her life and the things she had that she looked past my fathers imperfections. If you want to call human trafficking an imperfection. I can only assume that Mrs. Endlow does the same. The realization leaves a sour taste in my mouth but I continue my journey to the end of the hall where I can now hear Vin's low murmur.

"There's my favorite girl." His beautiful smile stretches across his face, his teeth sparkling in the LED lighting. He watches me walk through the door way and pulls out a chair for me.

"What the fuck are you doing here?" Theo spits at me. Blood already running down his face and over his crisp white long sleeve button down.

I put my hand out gesturing for the bat.

"Considering the positions we've both found ourselves in here, Theo, I think I'll ask the questions." My grin is sly.

Damn it feels good to speak without thinking. To say whatever I'm feeling without fear of consequence. That's just it, I'm no longer bound by repercussions or punishment for my actions. I can be whoever I want to be, whoever I am.

I don't have consequences with Vincenzo. As long as this man is my husband, my captor, my best friend, I don't have to be afraid of what men like Theodore and Brad Endlow are capable of. Because if anyone so much as looks at me the wrong way, he will bring a death so unkind upon them they will be reconsidering every life choice that has led them to that moment.

If that's not true love, I don't know what is.

Before him my life was a faint whisper of chaos and despair.

I was anxiously waiting for the other shoe to drop at all times, to be sucked down into a hole of self destruction so ravenous that it would consume me.

Vince shoved me off that ledge and I dove head first into a violent, love filled pool that I refuse to come back up from. I would follow this man anywhere, into any body of freezing, dark water as long as he was by my side.

I take the bat and swing it into Theodore's knee, so hard that the motion sends a residual vibration from my fingers up to my head and down to my toes, shattering it. I close my eyes and suck in a lungful of air. My chest rises and my ribs stretch.

That felt good.

So good that I repeat the same movement. His leg is limp and the only sound in the air are his muffled cries. Good thing he won't need that knee anymore.

"Sorry, Theo I've got a bit of pent up aggression toward this family." I let out a little giggle and continue. "Now that we've gotten that out of the way, I've got a couple questions for you?"

"You're fucking crazy!" He screams.

Typical man.

Of course I'm the crazy one for reacting to the many things this man has done to me and a multitude of others. "Let's not call names, I'm not a fan and you've still got one knee left. It could always be worse." I tap his other knee gently with the bat. "Did you kill Victoria?"

"No!" He shouts the word at me, not bothering to defend himself.

"Are you sure? It seems that you may have had a few reasons?"

As soon as I get the words out there's some commotion coming from up the stairs.

"Sounds like the Mrs. may be home?" Vince smirks at Theo.

"I'd hate to have to bring her in on the action."

Theodore screams.

"Where do your loyalties lie, Theodore? You clearly have no love for your wife, nor your mistress seeing how she and your unborn child are dead. Was it only Brad you cared for?" Vince asks with a sincere finality in his tone. "Or not even him? I haven't seen any missing person's reports yet."

"You know what what?" He continues on, not giving Theo a chance to respond. "Enzo, go put a bullet in her head. I don't feel like dealing with the shrieking."

Enzo puts his hand up to his forehead pretending to salute Vince. Before anyone speaks further he's racing out of the room and headed up the stairs to complete the task.

"Where were we, *Mio Amore*?" Vince asks me, his smile cold and calculated.

But the man bound to the chair in front of me speaks first. "I loved Victoria." His face is firm. He sounds sincere but I don't believe a man like him is capable of such a word.

"You don't seem shocked about the whole 'Unborn Child' thing? Is that why you killed her?"

Theo starts to sob. "I didn't kill her, Violet. I was trying to protect her. She found to many things out and she was going to go to the FBI. She had so much proof, so much evidence of what we'd been doing." He's rambling at this point and my blood feels thick under my skin.

The way he's talking about Vic like she was an inconvenience is wearing my patience thin.

"Did you or did you not shoot my fucking twin, Theodore?" I grit out between clenched teeth. I'm only second away from grinding my molars into dust.

"I didn't! I didn't, I swear!" He's crying so hard now he can barely get the words out in between breaths. "Please you have to believe me. It was- " Just before Theodore can spit the words out a piercing sound rings through the room and blood drips from the hole dead center in the middle of his forehead.

Vince and I turn in unison to see what the fuck is going on. In the door way is a man dressed in a plain white tee and blue denim jeans with a black ski mask over his face. His arms are free of any identifying marks.

Before either of us has a second to process the situation, a second shot rings out into the cold, concrete cell and Vince is crumpling to the ground before me. Everything is moving in slow motion as I turn and rush toward him.

I look up and the masked figure is gone.

All that's left is my husband bleeding out in my arms, the dead man tied to the metal chair, and the screaming that I can't seem to quiet.

36

Enzo

I make my way up the stairs to the sterile dining room. There's not a single thing in this house that would alert you to the fact a family lives here. I suppose they don't, only wolves in sheep's clothing lurk through these halls.

The two women in the room don't notice my entrance as they're a bit preoccupied. Alison Endlow holds tight to the girl's face, as if it's her fault she's restrained in a chair.

"What the fuck is going on in here?" She spits into her face.

The poor girl can't respond as she cries. I notice the bruises marring her perfectly porcelain skin and something screams to life inside of me.

"Yes, sweetheart, explain it to us. How did you tie yourself up? That's a party trick if I've ever seen one." She closes her eyes and let's the tears fall. There's something similar to relief on her face.

I'll let her feel that in this moment, because I am here to help her. However, she doesn't know what she's started with me. I plan to show her in full as soon as were done here.

"Who- who are you?" The old wench stutters at the sight of a rather large, strange man in her home.

"You can call me Enzo." My smile is wide, I show her every bright white tooth in my mouth. Unfortunately for her, fear is one of the most intoxicating emotions I've tasted yet. "I'd ask you the same, Alison, but we are already more acquainted than you know." I wink at her.

Alison backs away, screaming, and turns on her heel to head for the door. Before she can make more than three steps out of the room she hits the floor with a loud thud. I lower the gun back down and tuck it in my waist band.

Walking over to the gorgeous girl I had the pleasure of tying up only a little bit ago, I crouch down. "Now, my sweet little *Gattina*, what is your name?" I've been dying to ask since I laid my eyes on her. Like a lost little black cat, crossing my path at the most deliciously illogical time. I can tell that there is an air of ferocity about her, begging to be unleashed. I'm under a carefully woven spell I'm not sure she meant to cast.

When we entered the home, Theo slung over my shoulder with Vincenzo's gun to his head, she just stared. Maybe it was shock, maybe it was hope, I could never be sure. Between the vacant look in her eyes and the bruises on her skin, I knew no one in this house would be left breathing.

I've fucked more girls than I could count, I've dated and even had girlfriends. Never once during that time have I met a woman who intrigued me the way she has.

She doesn't know it yet but she's mine now.

"Ana." She whispers down to me, I can tell she's afraid but she's strong. This is just another day to her. It makes me wonder what her sky blue eyes have seen.

"Ana." I repeat back to her. "I'm Enzo."

"I heard." I chuckle at her response. She's funny, too? I might be in love.

She doesn't smile at her little joke but its funny nonetheless. I put my hand on her thigh, needing to ground myself into the moment, when a gunshot rings out faintly into the air.

For a split second I'm calm, until I remember that every gun we brought into this house has a silencer on it. I'm up and moving without a word as soon as the thought registers.

I sprint through the dark hallway to the cell that we put Theodore in. Near the chair Violet once sat in lays my brothers pale, bloody body. His head is resting on her lap while she sobs into his neck.

"Help him!" She screams at me. Both her hands are covered in bright red blood as she tries to stop the bleeding form the gaping hole in his chest.

I throw my arms under his shoulder to sit him up and then lift him by the waist to throw him over my shoulder the same way we brought Theodore down here.

"Go untie Ana!" I shout to Violet. My brother is heavy as fuck but I'll damned if he dies in this basement today.

She's reluctant to leave Vince at first but she knows we can't leave her like that. She runs up the stairs ahead of me as I focus on getting Vin to the SUV. By the time I've made it to the front door Violet is right behind me.

I reach into my pocket and throw my phone to Vi.

"Call the doctor, tell him what happened and to meet us at the cabin." Her hands shake as she scrolls my contacts and presses 'Doc' reciting exactly what I told her.

After I throw Vince in the back seat I turn to head for the drivers seat and make contact with my newest obsession. "We'll be back, *Gattina*."

Ana lowers her eyes and shuts the door. I shut mine and race down the drive way to the gate that leads to the road, I don't have time to read into that right now.

I've always thought of my big brother as invincible but that was a lot of fucking blood and knowing Vince, he'd die out of spite.

Just to prove me wrong.

37

Vincenzo

The small, warm hands on my face feel like home. When they rake up through my messy hair I know they are keeping me tethered to the world right now. I keep thinking how easy it would be to just let go. I could let the overwhelming sleep take me over and be done with it all.

The pain that I've carried with me since my sister was taken. The pain I felt when I woke up from a coma and learned that my mother had taken her own life. The physical pain I've brought on myself weeding out the undesirable of the world. So many tragic things that will follow me until I'm no longer earth side.

Even with that weight upon my shoulders, I've never felt as light as I have with Violet. I can't leave her here to deal with this alone. She's been alone too long, I won't do it.

I use the last ounce of energy I feel coursing through me to open my eyes.

"I love you, Violet."

38

Violet

I hold back the tears as we fly down the back roads to the secluded cabin in the woods. When we pull up there's already a small blue sports car parked in the gravel driveway. The short older man that took care of me, after my little hostage stunt, steps out as we pull in.

"Gun shot wound to the chest." Enzo barks out at the man, carrying his big brother up to the front door. Vin obviously can't unlock the door at the moment so Enzo sends a steel toed boot flying into the wooden door. Once, twice, and then the door breaks free of the hinges and falls to the ground. He steps right on it as Dr. Partello and I follow closely behind.

"On the table." The doctor gestures toward the dining area. Enzo swings his arm over it, sending all of its contents crashing to the ground and lays his brother down on the table as gentle but quickly as possible.

I'm at Vincenzo's side in a blink, kissing his forehead and neck. Checking for the faint pulse of his heart with my lips. All of the color has left his skin and his lips are turning a grayish color as time drags on. I hold his hand in mine for what I think may be the first time ever.

I've lived 18 years never knowing him but I don't think I could do even one more without. I've turned into the girls I hate, the kind that say they'd die with out their significant other because I don't think that, I know it.

"Go upstairs, Violet." Enzo's face is serious and his tone unrelenting.

"I can't leave him, Enzo. Don't ask that of me." I plead with him but I can tell it's not working.

Vince twitches on the table beneath us. I'm not sure if he can hear us but I don't want him spending precious energy stressing about me when he's fighting for his life. My brother in law's face softens but is still stony. He doesn't have time for me either.

"Okay." I bring my lips down to Vince's soft, plump ones. "I love you, Vincenzo."

And then I make my way upstairs.

It's only been an hour but it feels like three as I've laid on the uncomfortable bed in the spare room up here. The feel in the room is very cabin-y. I don't hate it but its definitely not my style. The blanket on the bed is old and scratchy with a flannel print.

I've counted the tree's outside the window a hundred times. I count until I'm not sure if I've counted the same one twice or not, and then I start over. The bright yellow, oranges, and vibrant reds keep my heart still. I focus on the small things that this place has brought me. Coloring over those exact leaves in art class back in elementary school, running through the woods with friends, s'mores around a campfire at 6th grade camp.

I'm sure I've felt happiness more times than that in my life but the memories are few and far between. Long gone and lost by the darkness that dances in my consciousness. Those memories are nothing compared to the contentment that Vince brings me. Places in my brain that I thought had been cauterized by constant mental discomfort were resurrected by the positive emotions and caring I've experienced from this man and his family.

My family.

I've used this time to ponder the situation and I know what I have to do.

There was something familiar about the man in the basement at the Endlow's. It's only a theory but I think I know who killed Theo and shot my husband. I can't tell them until Vincenzo is well and that could be days, weeks. I'm going to have handle this one myself.

I sit up from the bed and spend a few seconds staring at the door. An eerie calmness comes over me as I feel everything settle in to place. Something in my bones tells me Vince will be okay. Enzo is here to care for him. I'm sure Dr. Partello's life depends on his survival. Not to mention there is no one stronger than Vince.

The last thing the devil needs is a competitor like Vincenzo coming down to threaten his position.

Stealthily, I sneak down the stairs and out the back door. I'm lucky the door isn't unnecessarily squeaky, nor are the steps leading to the ground. I crouch down, careful not to be seen in the windows at the front of the house as I hop into the drivers seat of the Tahoe and turn it on.

I glance up to see that the men are still focused on Vincenzo and have no idea the truck is running. I put it in reverse and creep down the long driveway, not taking my eyes off the scene in front of me.

I make it to the end without a hitch and head off in the direction of the city. I race down the old roads and into town. I hardly stop for the lights as I've only got one thing on my mind right now.

I've got this grave feeling that I'll be killing two birds with one stone when I confront the man that shot my husband. How ironic would that be? Losing the two most important people in my life to the same person over circumstances I never saw coming.

I wait at the end of the road for a while before a familiar white Mercedes Benz pulls into the circle drive six or seven houses down. I hold my hands over my mouth as the same blue jeans step out of the car, followed by an identical white tee shirt. Not a speck of my husbands blood on the crisp cotton.

My blood boils as he pats his hair into place in the side mirror before sauntering up to the front door and letting himself in. I put the Tahoe in drive and make my way to the house.

I pull right up into the front yard as close as I can get to the door and throw the SUV into park. I step out and feel for the knife at my thigh, once I confirm it's placement I reach into the seat and grab the gun I stole on my way out of the cabin.

I've been mistreated by these people, dehumanized and sold off without a second thought. I may not have forgiven them but I've come terms with the circumstances that come along with being a girl in my world. What I refuse to reason with is the harming of my husband.

I will burn this fucking world down for him.

I march to the front door and bust through, grateful it's unlocked. I'm not sure I could do the whole kick thing and I'm grateful I'm not stuck trying it out.

VIOLET

The house is quiet. I'm sure my dad is upstairs, getting ready to shower and change. He never dresses casually. I'm also sure my mom is passed out drunk somewhere, the house is never this quiet when she's conscious.

I pad my way up the stairs and head straight to his room. My path changes when I hear a whispered voice coming from the office my father spend all of his time in when he's home. The door is slightly ajar and I peek through the gap to see him sitting at the desk staring into desktop computer screen, shouldering his cell to his ear. He looks a bit worried as he types at full speed.

I guess maybe he's feeling a bit guilty about murdering his business partner in cold blood. It seems like he'd be a bit more excited about being the sole proprietor of the business now. I suppose there will be some questions but he's always been so deviously deceptive I'm sure he'll figure it out.

I push the door open slowly and step inside. I smile and wave. "Hi, dad." I can't imagine what I look like right now. My leggings are damp and starting to stiffen from Vin's blood. I'm sure my messy bun is mostly just 'mess' at the moment. My face is bare except for the expensive moisturizer my husband had imported from Italy.

All things my father and ex-fiancee simply would not accept. For years I've been forced to wear uncomfortable clothes, thickly caked makeup, and pristine updo's. Bright eye looks and clothes to match. I couldn't even read the books I wanted to read because they're 'for whores'. I can't fathom the life I used to live compared to the life I live now. Free to think and feel however and whatever I want.

And right now I'm feeling rather murderous.

My father's eyes rove over my body frantically. "What are

you doing here?"

"Well that's not the warm welcome I was expecting." I let out a little laugh. "I mean it's been how long since we last saw each other?" Only a few hours now but I'm sure he doesn't think I'm capable of figuring that out. Or confronting him, at least.

He stares up at me as I walk my way toward him.

"Tell me, Winston, did you look for your only remaining daughter? Or did you decide you were better off without the hassle."

"Of course I looked for you!" His voice breaks a bit as he tries to find the right words to comfort me, to stop the palpable mental break down from slowly creeping up on me.

I pout my lips and use a sincere tone of voice. "I mean what's the point if I'm not here to marry Brad? What would set you apart from any of Theo's other business partners?"

"Violet, you don't know what you're talking about. I don't know what that man has told you, but it's not true." He tries to smile, as if I don't know exactly what I'm talking about.

"But I do. I know exactly what I'm talking about. I know that I'm just a pawn in this little game you've been playing with Theo. I know he was having an affair with Victoria who was pregnant with your grandchild." I'm breathing heavily now as I start to raise my voice. "I know that you put her down like a fucking dog at that party and you let me believe she killed herself this entire time!" I scream at him. I can't help myself as the rage over takes me.

While the emotions are swirling inside of me begging to break free, I manage to keep them at bay until I see him scramble for his top drawer.

I close the distance quickly, bringing my self to his desk. I land at the front, letting my knife glide through the air. I bring it down and nail his hand to the rich mahogany colored wood. His scream is loud and sharp bringing a sick pleasure to the forefront of my brain.

I let go of the knife and watch the blood puddle under and above his hand, bringing a smile to my face. "I guess we'll all bleed today, huh?"

"I don't get it, Winston?" I sit down in the chair next to me, in front of him. Pulling the pistol from my waist band I tap it to my chin. "Why kill Victoria, wasn't that another line of indefinite linkage to the Endlow family?"

"You are insane just like your fucking mother." I let a giggle bubble out from between my lips. That's not the dig he thinks it is. My mother is far from insane. An addict? An adulterer? A terrible mother? All of the above. But I wouldn't exactly call her insane, i mean look at this beautiful house she lives in. She's never worked a day in her life, only drives expensive sports cars, and wears all designer clothing. In another life I'd call her genius, except all of this was paid for by the blood and tears of unwilling young women, including my twin.

Perhaps I should show him what insane looks like.

I raise the gun to his forehead. "That's not an answer, father." I drop the grin. "Tell me why you killed my sister before I put a bullet between your eyes."

"He wanted to leave." He spits bluntly, not even bothering to imitate a fatherly emotion. "I don't have the clientele Theo has. I can't run this business without him."

"Well that's unfortunate since the whole family is dead."

"He was going to take her away from you anyways, don't you see that? They were going to run off somewhere and you would have never seen her again." The look of disgust on his face is chilling. "You've always been reasonable, Violet. Look at the bigger picture hear. Whether I participate in the trade or not, it will still take place." He tries to reason with me. "You went with brad and never complained a single time. You acted exactly how an acceptable wife would. Victoria wasn't like you. She was a whore. If she knew how to keep her legs shut none of us would be in this position right now."

He tries to change his tone into something more sincere, nurturing. "You know what it was like when she was home, Vi. All she did was cause problems for us." He's got a sad smirk on his face trying to play on my emotions. "She saw some stuff she shouldn't have, honey. This is all too much for you little girls to understand. She wanted her own father sent to prison, locked up for life."

I want to smirk, I want to throwback my head back in laughter, mostly I want to blow his fucking brains out. But I refrain. This guy is in so deep that he can't tell his ass from a hole in the ground. He refers to Victoria and I as children, yet has no problem selling women our same age. I mean, shit, he basically gave me away for free. Both of our parents forced us to grow up long before it was time.

He's become so corrupted by wealth and power that there is no reasoning with him. There is no right and wrong, no second or third place. It's everything or nothing.

He makes my husband look like a saint.

Maybe in his own fucked up way, he is.

I've heard enough. He confessed to taking the life of my sister and niece or nephew, he confessed to his part in this sex trafficking ring that's run rampant in our small town, and he confessed to his plans for me.

Little did he know, bartering me off to live in my own fucked up version of hell these last couple of years would turn into the wild twist of events that would seal his fate. I walk to the other side of the desk and sit directly in front of my father. He tries to back away but winces at the pain in his hand.

He's trapped.

"I'm sorry, dad." I return his same sad smile. I can tell he believes it with the look of relief on his face. "I'm sorry that you thought so little of me. That you though I was so weak I wouldn't be able to avenge my sister and husband."

His face twists in confusion. I swing the gun down across my fathers face and watch the blood spray across the room, coating his shirt and pants that should have been painted by my husbands blood but he's too weak to step that close. Too feeble to put his hands on a man he knows he wouldn't win against. Power flows through me as I bring the gun down on his skull again and again. The only thing keeping his body up is his hand still stuck into the desk. Brain matter leaks from his head while I continue to let my rage fuel my movements. This is the only retribution my twin will be given and I intend to pay it in full.

When I'm sure he's no longer breathing I wipe the sweat and blood from my eyes with the back of my hand. I pull the beautiful blade Noelle gave me from his pale hand and wipe both sides off on my thigh, resheathing it.

I turn and walk toward the door. I walk up the stairs toward my parents room and am not shocked at the sight in front of me. Throughout the screaming and mayhem I just brought upon this house my mother is passed out in her luxury king sized bed, on Egyptian cotton sheets, and in a brand name dress wrapped tightly around the body she bought.

I'll leave Winston for her to find. She can wail over her body the same way I did Victoria's. She can try and clean him up the same way I did her. I don't give it another thought before I shut the door and head for my car.

The bond of blood is so insignificant when you know what it's like to be bound by choice.

By love and desire, self preservation and trust.

39

Vincenzo

I lay in the warm room, engulfed in my favorite scent with the sun shining over my face. I blink my eyes open and glance around. At first I don't process the situation. It's certainly not uncommon to wake up at home and in bed.

Quickly, I sit up and wince at the movement. My chest is bandaged and it hurts to inhale too deeply. I look around the room but Violet isn't there. I can smell her but that does little to quiet the panic brewing inside of me.

At once the memories all come rushing back to me. We were in St. Lane, we were torturing information out of Theodore, and then we weren't. I rack my brain trying to remember exactly what happened last night. How are we back on the island already? Who drove the boat?

Before I chalk it up to insanity, my wife comes striding into the room with her hair wrapped up in a towel and one of her signature pair's of silky sleep wear.

"You're awake!" She rushes over to me, wrapping her arms around me gently. "I was getting worried."

I look over Violet's face. Okay, I'm fucking confused.

"It's been 8 days, Vin! Dr. Partello just took you off the sedatives and feeding tube last night. Can you eat? I'll be right back!" She goes to jump up from the bed but I grab her wrist.

"8 days?" I scrunch my brows at her.

Her giggle is music to my hears. "Yeah, we have some catching up to do." She leans in to plant a kiss on my cheek.

I grab her with one hand and turn my face to hers. I don't give her time before I crash my lips into hers. I may have been dead to the world but my body hasn't forgotten how long it's been since I've been inside of her.

I lay back and pull her down on top of me but she doesn't cooperate.

"Vincenzo, absolutely not. You just woke up! You've got a bullet wound in your chest!" She's smiling but her tone is serious. It's cute that she thinks a little hole in my chest could ever stop me from fucking her.

I give her another hard tug and her elbows give out. The silk of her tank is warm and I can feel her pebbled nipple press into me. "I've missed you, *Amore Mio.*" I whisper into her ear as I suck the lobe into my mouth.

"I'm on my period, I can't." I almost want to be sad at the revelation there is no baby inside of her but I smile at the fact she thinks that would deter me.

"My favorite lube." I wink up at her.

"You're sick." She lowers her head down on to me trying to hide the blush on her cheeks. I feel her smile into my chest and I continue down her throat sucking at the delicate skin covering her clavicle.

Violet leans up to slide the covers down and throw a leg over my hips, straddling me. I palm both of her round cheeks, giving them a firm squeeze.

"Take it out, Violet." She slides her small hand into my boxers. Her palm is soft as she struggles to circle it around me.

"Just like that, *Mio Angelo*." She backs her knees up until her ass is resting against my thighs. Her head lowers and she takes me into her hot mouth. "Fuck, Vi."

Her head bobs as she sucks me into the back of her throat. I'm running on little to no energy so I'm lazy with my thrusts. She moans and it sends a delectable yet irritating vibration down to my balls.

"Enough. Ride my cock." I need it now. I can't go another moment without her tight pussy wrapped around me.

She makes a show of stripping her tank top and shorts off. Her beautiful milky skin is mostly healed of its cuts and the wings under her tits look perfect. My wife is a masterpiece in every sense of the word.

She throws her blonde locks to the side over her shoulder as she crawls up my body to meet my lips. I let her take control of our kiss, my need to devour her lessened a fraction with the insistent pain in my chest. I lay my head back and let her pepper kisses down my throat and over the spot where a bullet entered my chest a little over a week ago. I growl in dissatisfaction letting her no my patience is wearing thin.

I grab her hips with a roughness I know she can handle, a firmness she craves and use the moment to slide into her. She lowers herself down over me until I'm fully seated inside her.

We pant in unison at the sensation I know we've both missed so much. Slowly, she rocks her hips back and forth on top of me. I run my hand up her soft abdomen and over her breast, pinching her nipple. I continue up over her chest until my hand surrounds her fragile neck.

Violet grips the wrist closest to her face with one hand and grabs my shoulder with the other. Her rhythm never falters as she pushes down hard, driving me as deep into her as she can. I use my free hand to grip her ass.

I push up into her and squeeze her throat until her lips pop open. "Take what you need from me, *bellisima*." I'm barely able to grit the words between my teeth, lost somewhere in the middle of pleasure and pain.

"Fucking come, Violet." Her hips jerk incessantly at the demand.

I apply more pressure to her throat and she tips her head back in ecstasy until I feel her muscles milking me. I pull her lips down to mine chasing right behind her. We come together with our tongues as deep as we can get them.

Unfortunately, now that I've appeased the unabating need to be inside of her, I'm having much more sobering thoughts.

I want to ask her what the fuck happened. How are we home? Where is Theodore? Who shot me?

But I don't. She can tell me over breakfast in a little bit.

"Where do you want to go, Violet?" She scrunches her brows in the adorable way she always does as she rolls off me.

"You're admissions essay for St. Lane University. You said you wanted to travel after school. Where are we going?"

She rolls her eyes in typical Violet Elaine Bianchi fashion, painting a beautiful smile across her lips.

"Surprise me."

40

Violet

After Vince takes his seat at the island next to me, I turn to face him. "Do you remember what happened in the basement?"

"I think so. I remember a bullet hole through Theodore's head and then I passed out." I grab my fork more that ready to work my way into the French toast sitting in front of me.

"It was my father." I try to keep my voice steady. I don't regret killing him or Brad but the guilt of the act itself has weighed heavy over me the last few weeks. "I recognized him almost immediately but I had to make sure you were okay. I thought you were going to die." My voice shakes as I feel my appetite retreating.

"It's okay Violet, I will find him." Vince reaches out to stroke the skin on the back of my hand. Sometimes it's hard to picture him as a murderer, other times it's hard to see him as a lover. Now that we share the first title, it's been easier to correlate the two.

"There's no need, Vin." He drops his fork onto his plate with a loud clang. He stares into my eyes with a look I've come to know as agitation. He thinks I want to keep him alive. "I killed him."

He doesn't speak so I continue. "He confessed to everything, he told me he knew Victoria was pregnant and killed her anyway." I lower my eyes back to my food as I push it around my plate.

"He told me that Theodore and Victoria were going to runaway together to start their family, Theo was telling the truth."

"I'm glad that you know, but it doesn't change anything." Vince's voice is strong and steady as he pulls me into him, wrapping me in warmth. "He still bought and sold off young girls like they were cattle. Whether he had a change of heart or not he still stole my sister away from her home, along with countless other children."

"I know, it's just a lot. I don't feel bad any of these people are dead. I wish my sister was here. I wish I could meet my niece or nephew. I wish you're sister was here. I just wish things were different." He sweeps my hair out my face gaining my attention once more.

"I know." Softness radiates from his tone. Vince knows exactly how to settle the sea that's always a second away from seizing the ship inside my head. "Things will be different. You have nothing but time and resources to figure out how you're going to change the world, Vi."

After breakfast Vince walks me down to the pole barn so we can ride in the side by side. I told him all about Enzo and how he helped save his life, I know that his little brother would never mention it.

VIOLET

We coast lazily along the shore line and through the trees on the way to Enzo's side of the island. Vince's points out some of his favorite areas of the island and we talk about the different animals he's come across. None of which were bears or wolves. Only small critters and the occasional fox or coyote.

We pull up to the basement and my husband lets himself in without so much as bothering to knock. "Enzo!" He shouts as we pad our way up the stairs and into the kitchen. I haven't been back since I was running from Vince but the thought only sends a current straight to my core.

"Come out, come out wherever you are!" I shout after him. My husband's little brother loves a good game.

But nothing

No laughter or sarcastic jokes, the house is doused in quiet and tranquility. Two things Enzo is not quite capable of.

Vincenzo pulls his phone out and I know he's calling his brother. After just a few rings he picks up and I realize he's on speaker.

"Hello? Where the hell are you?" I smirk and Enzo laughs at the concern laced into Vin's tone.

"Michigan. Big brother, you seem concerned? Glad to see you're alive and well. You're welcome."

I laugh and Vince shoots me a look. I shrug my shoulders and sit at the table in the dining room, enjoying the view.

"No, I just like to no who comes and goes from my island. Why are you in Michigan?"

Pure malevolence shines through in Enzos next response. "Hunting, brother. Got to go now." The line goes dead and I have a feeling I know exactly what or who Enzo is hunting.

I don't let on as my husband makes a questioning face in my direction. I told Vincenzo mostly everything from the time he was unconscious. I told him exactly what I did to Winston Woodruff and what he told me. For some reason, at the time, the tension between Enzo and Ana didn't seem noteworthy. Now, in hindsight, I'm wondering if maybe I was a bit wrapped up in the moment and something slipped my radar.

"I don't know?" I try my new poker face as I move to the fridge. "Lets drink all of his alcohol and leave."

Vince laughs. "We'd be here for days if we tried that." He pulls me into the crook of his arm and kisses the top of my head.

"Let's go, we need to pack."

I don't respond, I just smile up into the beautiful face of my captor.

My lover, my husband.

My best friend.

41

Vincenzo

6 months later

Violet steps out of the outdoor shower with her gorgeous body on display. Her golden skin drips as she walks over to lay on the sun chair next to me. We've spent the entire day back and forth between the ocean, the secluded beach, and the private hut I purchased just for us.

We've been on vacation for 6 months but yesterday we landed in Bali. Her only request in out travel plans was to spend her birthday here. For 186 days we've danced and drank and fucked our way across the globe. Staying in touristy areas and off the grid, whatever suits our mood.

We've stayed in lavish hotels and cozy huts with some of the locals. We've eaten meals prepared by five star Michelin chefs and shared some over an open fire on the beach.

Before we left I put Violet's birth control back into her bathroom so I could give her this experience. I wouldn't call it a noble gesture considering I messed with it in the first place but it took a lot of self fucking control to put it back.

"We have reservations, *Amore Mio*." I sit up and stroke my hand over the naked, velvety flesh of her stomach. My accent has thickened due to a new level of comfortability with my wife and time spent back home in Italy. "You might want to put some clothes on before you make us late." I can feel my eyes darken as they rove over her body, suddenly I'm not so hungry.

Not for food.

"Then, we'll be late." The giant diamond ring I gave her this morning threatens to blind me as she puts her arms up over her head, laying back flat. Her breasts sway with the movement and that's all the invitation I need before I am up and removing my swim trunks.

"The birthday girl is feeling particularly naughty today, I see." The sun sets behind us and the colors illuminate that familiar silvery glow in her eyes. Her skin is clear and beautiful, her eyes well rested, her smile genuine.

She's got a sly grin on her face as I push both of her knees up roughly and sink deep inside of her. "Happy Birthday, *Mio Angelo*."

I grab a fist full of Violet's hair and pull her head up, not only giving me some stability as I thrust into her ruthlessly but so we can watch together as I fuck her. Over and over I pound into her, she doesn't dare look away from where we meet.

She's such a good fucking girl.

We never do make those reservations.

Printed in Great Britain
by Amazon